SEDNA

Richard L. Smith

ISBN: 978-1-943767-88-5

Other books by Richard L. Smith

Time Lacuna	2003	Authorhouse	ISBN 1-4107-8383-0
Out of China	2005	Xulon	ISBN 1-59781-502-0
New Eden	2009	iUniverse	ISBN 1-4401-0781-8
Powerless	2011	iUniverse	ISBN 1-4620-5365-0 and -5367-4 and -5366-7

Contents

Preface

I have often wondered about those technological wonders that would be available to science fiction writers a hundred years from now. Given the progress technology experienced in the past seventy years, forecasting technology available one hundred years from now is apt to come up far short of reality. Jules Vern was an exceptional nineteenth century prophet whose novels predicted nuclear submarines, space travel, and television among many other wonders of our modern world. I do not have the extraordinary vision of a Jules Vern, but Sedna is a story of exploration and discovery that takes place in the twenty-second century and, in this novel, I attempt to imagine the technological background necessary to make the novel plausible.

Sedna is the story of a geological team that make the long journey through our solar system to explore a remote dwarf planet named Sedna, an enigmatic icy world seventy-six times further away from the sun than is our Earth and a planet that challenges accepted theories about the formation of our solar system. Initially, the scientific team decided that Sedna must be an oddball and did not attempt to study the dwarf planet. In the late twenty-first century, the United World Science Foundation (UWSF) built an observatory on Sedna as a platform to study the outer reaches of our solar system. In 2117, the Foundation funded a team of geologists and scientists to answer some of the enigmatic mysteries of this small, unusual dwarf planet wrapped in enigmas that demand answers. The novel follows these scientists as they journey through the solar system, relates their explorations on Sedna, their discovery of "something wonderful," and their long delayed journey home.

Chapter One
The Invitation

UC Professor and Geologist Dr. Gerald (Jerry) Abrams sat in his University of California—Berkeley office trying to make sense of the data displayed on his computer screen. Jerry had recently returned from a November 2116 expedition to the Antarctic Ice sheet where he worked with a team of other geologists collecting meteorites. The desert plains of Antarctica were an ideal place to collect these visitors from space. With so little snowfall, any meteorite remained close to or even on the surface. In a box of samples that he collected, one sample in particular had captured his attention. Jerry had collected several small meteorites before this potato-size rock caught his attention. While most of the meteorites he had found were stony-iron or carbonaceous chondrites, back at camp this particular sample defied classification. Reddish brown, shaped like an Idaho potato with Swiss cheeses-like holes, the mineral content consisted of graphite, olivine, and other carbon molecules. He initially thought the meteorite was a member of the primitive achrondrite Ureilite family, but when back at his office at the UC Berkley, the mineralogical analysis suggested this specimen did not fit that or any other particular classification. Most astounding, the radiometric and isotopic results indicated the sample was over seven billion years old, predating our own solar system. Had he discovered an example of a meteorite that originated in another distant and much older solar system? If so, it would pique the interest of geologists and astronomers alike. Jerry printed out a copy of the mineralogical, isotopic, and radiometric dating tests and with the meteorite and a glass slide sample, hurried over to the office of his astronomer friend, Dr. Wendy Wilson.

Wendy was a trim forty-year-old honey-blond who specialized in searching for and describing trans-Neptunian objects (TNOs)—that is, objects beyond the orbit of Neptune. Jerry and Wendy had been close since then their post-doc days at Caltech several years ago. He knew she would be keenly interested in his meteorite. Wendy responded to the knock on her office door with a friendly "Come in," and when she recognized Jerry she greeted him with a warm smile and a hug reminiscent of their former relationship.

Wendy asked in a mocking way, "What prompts that Cheshire Cat smile on your face, Jerry, and what's that in your hand?"

Jerry handed the meteorite to her, along with the glass slide sample and a printout of the computer data. She put on a pair of gloves and examined the meteorite, turning it repeatedly in her hands. Then she looked over the isotopic and radiometric data, and then placed the glass slide sample under her microscope. After a couple of minutes, she looked from the microscope and sighed.

"There is no doubt in my mind that this meteorite is unique and defies classification, yet can you be sure of this isotopic data? It is hard to believe that this rock is over 7 billion years old. Perhaps you should repeat those tests."

"I already have done so … three times," Jerry said, "and each time the results are the same. The radiometric dating confirms that this meteorite is older than our solar system."

Wendy looked again at the data. "I don't believe meteorite hunters have ever found a sample whose origin can be definitively traced to another solar system. If your analysis is correct, you have made a truly astounding discovery. You should take the sample and resulting data to Dr. Josh Vincent at Caltech. I understand the United World Science Foundation (UWSF) has given him a generous grant and he is now organizing a geological expedition to Sedna. I'm sure he would be very interested in examining your meteorite."

Jerry knew Dr. Josh Vincent well. He had been Jerry's doctorate adviser at Caltech and they had remained friends ever since. "Dr. Vincent is organizing an expedition to Sedna?" Jerry said, surprised. "That little ice rock in the outer reaches of our Solar System? What possible interest does Dr. Vincent have with Sedna?"

Dr. Josh Vincent was a world-renowned UWSF geologist, but his interest was in Earth geology, not astronomy.

"Yes … Sedna," Wendy said. "Josh will want to see this meteorite firsthand, and while you are there ask him about the Sedna geological expedition."

Thanking Wendy for her advice, Jerry went back to his office and called Dr. Vincent, who immediately invited him to come down to Caltech and bring his meteorite with him.

The next day Jerry's wife, Carol, drove him to Fremont where he boarded the maglev train to downtown Los Angeles. After the one-hour train ride, he caught the subway to Caltech in Pasadena. Knocking on Dr. Vincent's office door, he entered and found Josh in a meeting with another scientist. They were discussing details of the expedition to Sedna. Both men stood up when Jerry entered the room, and Dr. Vincent smiled and shook Jerry's hand.

"Jerry, it's good to see you again. Let me introduce Dr. Isake Mitera, an associate geologist and mineralogist and a member of our Sedna geological team."

Jerry shook hands with Dr. Mitera and remembered his many articles on the geology of asteroids, now routinely mined for their minerals.

"We have been discussing the expedition to Sedna in September," Dr. Vincent said. "How goes it at Berkeley and how was your trip to Antarctica?"

Jerry frowned. "Berkeley is as always a hotbed of controversy, but the meteorite expedition to Antarctica was very productive. I brought along a most unusual meteorite that I found on that expedition, the one that we spoke about on the phone yesterday. I also have the computer analysis and a microscope slide from it." He took the potato-size meteorite out of his backpack and placed it on Dr. Vincent's desk. Dr. Vincent examined the meteorite and then handed the sample to Dr. Mitera. He asked for the sample slide and placed it under his microscope, then invited Isake to have a look.

"This sample defies classification," Dr. Vincent said and asked Dr. Mitera for his expert opinion.

"The closest family likeness would be the primitive achrondrites, perhaps the Ureilites, yet mineralogically it doesn't belong to any known family," Dr. Mitera said. "Most astounding is the radiometric dating that claims this sample is older than our solar system."

Dr. Vincent then handed the computer data to Dr. Mitera to examine. Dr. Mitera remained as inscrutable as ever after his examination.

"This data points out a very unusual ratio of carbon 12 to carbon 14," Isake finally commented, "which proves the sample must be 6–7 billion years old."

He turned to Jerry. "I assume you reran these tests."

"Yes, I did ... three times over," Jerry answered.

"Dr. Vincent, what is your opinion?" Isake asked.

"I think if Dr. Abrams doesn't mind, we should repeat the isometric and mineralogical analysis in our own laboratories," Josh suggested.

Then he turned to Jerry and said, "Meanwhile, if you can hang around for another day, tomorrow I am giving a lecture on Sedna and our expedition to that dwarf planet and I would like you to attend. This icy rock is an enigma wrapped in a mystery. While only about one-half the diameter of Pluto, it has a mass equal to Pluto's and a density greater than that of Mercury. Its elliptical orbit lies outside the plane of our solar system and now sits at a 76 astronomical unit perihelion where it arrived in 2076. At an Aphelion of 700 astronomical units, it is so far away from the sun that it is only observable when near perihelion, a position it will enjoy for another 300 years. Sedna is an oddity that defies explanation, an eccentric member of the trans-Neptune objects (TNO) that include Pluto and Eris. After the United World Science Association (UWSF) first set foot on Sedna thirty years ago, they determined it would make an ideal platform from which to study the outer solar system. The International Astronomical Union (IAU, a division of UWSF) funded the observatory project and chose the largest crater on the planet, the 10-mile-wide Gamma Crater, as the location for the Sedna International Observatory (SIO). After ten years of construction, the SIO 30-meter segmented telescope saw first light this decade. Within a year, the SIO team began making important discoveries about the outer solar system. Yet the SIO astronomers and construction engineers showed little interest in solving the many geological mysteries of their host planet and as far as I know, no one has ever ventured beyond the Gamma Crater floor." Dr. Vincent paused.

"Only recently, the unusual geology and orbit of this little planet finally drew the interest the UWSF. Last fiscal year they funded a geological expedition to Sedna and hired me to organize and explore Sedna and perhaps answer some of its mysteries. I am now recruiting expedition team members and organizing the mission. Tomorrow's lecture may interest you in this geological expedition to Sedna."

The offer intrigued Jerry and he committed to stay over and attend Dr. Vincent's lecture. The lecture took place in the Hubble Auditorium, where by 1:45 there wasn't an empty seat. At exactly 2:00 PM, Dr. Vincent strode to the podium, surveyed his audience, and began the lecture.

"On its discovery early in the twenty-first century, the International Astronomical Union (IAU) named 2003 BD12 'Sedna,' after the Inuit goddess of the frozen Arctic Ocean. Sedna is one of the larger members of the distant Kuiper Belt of dwarf planets that include Pluto and Eris. Although it has been over a hundred years since Sedna's discovery and despite placing the first explorers on its surface thirty years ago, this minor planet remains an enigma wrapped in mystery. Its elliptical orbit around the sun ranges from 76 AU (one AU is the distance from Earth to the sun or 93 million miles) to over 700 AU. Now in 2117 the dwarf planet is moving away from its perihelion, the closest approach to the sun in its 11,400-year orbit. This distant icy rock is so remote that even our fastest starship requires a thirty-one-month journey through the solar system to arrive on its surface. Only during the 300-yearlong summer will the planet remain accessible. At its present 77AU distance, the sun can only raise the surface temperature to a frigid 238 degrees centigrade below zero. In a couple of hundred years, Sedna's surface temperature will drop to only a few degrees above absolute zero. Despite the frigid summer temperature, the sun provides enough warmth to sublimate nitrogen and methane from the surface and form a tenuous yet ephemeral atmosphere." Dr. Vincent paused for a few seconds and took a sip of water.

"Fifteen years ago, the UWSF began construction of a 30-meter telescope on Sedna and ever since then astronomy, not geology, has been the scientific focus—that is, until Sedna captured the undivided attention of the UWSF geological society two years ago. With a diameter of 1100 miles, Sedna is only half the diameter of Pluto or Eris, yet its density is greater than that of Mercury. It is the densest body in the solar system with a gravitational field greater than its small size should dictate. The discovery of a magnetic field points to the presence of a dense yet molten nickel-iron core that provides a source of internal heat, perhaps due to radioactive decay. The hemisphere where the UWSF chose to build the SIO is similar to that of many other moons, including our own satellite. It is rocky, pitted by craters, and gray with a low albedo. The opposite hemisphere is different: mostly flat, reddish in color, and almost lacking in craters."

Dr. Vincent paused to project a slowly rotating holograph of Sedna taken from one hundred thousand miles.

"The strangely different Sedna hemispheres add to the enigma. One side looks like our moon, while the other side looks like Mars. Two parallel 1200-meter-high mountain ranges, named the Walnut Mountains, circle the entire planet from the north to south poles, and separate the different hemispheres from each other. In the holograph, Sedna reminds one of a walnut, hence the mountain ranges' given name. The best theory is that two separate bodies slammed into each other and melted to form the planet."

Dr. Vincent then showed a slide depicting Sedna's orbit about the Sun.

"Sedna's exaggerated elliptical orbit outside the plane of the solar system implies that it might not be an original member of our solar system, but a kidnapped member from a visiting star. Because of the unimaginable remoteness of even the nearest star solar system, Proxima Centauri, its planets remain inaccessible to humans. If indeed Sedna arrived from another solar system, then a study of its surface could provide valuable information about a former member of a distant star."

Dr. Vincent paused to take a sip of water.

"Normally such a barren and distant dwarf planet wouldn't capture the attention of IAU astronomers. Nevertheless, after the first astronauts set foot on Sedna in 2086, the IAU decided that because of its remoteness and low gravity, Sedna would be ideally suited to host an observatory to search for rogue members of the outer solar system and to study other star systems. In 2101, the IAU funded the Sedna Interstellar Observatory, or SIO, and after fifteen years of planning and construction, in 2114 the new telescope achieved first light and immediately made an important discovery.

"For many years, the orbits of several TNO dwarf planets suggested that some other large 'planet X' or a distant companion to our sun, perhaps a brown or red dwarf, could be out there tugging on them. After many years searching for this elusive body using Earth, moon, and space-based telescopes, astronomers had discovered hundreds of dwarf TNO planets like Pluto and Eris and the recently discovered remote Kuiper Belt planet Leto, a body about the size of Mercury yet over 100 AU's beyond the sun. Yet even Leto did not fully explain some of the TNO orbits. Many believed there must be a distant companion to our Sun, possibly a small red dwarf star whose gravity is tugging on Neptune and TNOs. Then in 2115 the SIO discovered Nemesis, a red dwarf star only 120 times the mass of Jupiter, yet massive enough to allow its core to fuse deuterium into helium and produce a glowing surface temperature of two thousand degrees. Orbiting outside the plane of our solar system at 2,300 AU, it was little wonder that this dim companion remained undetected until the SIO saw first light from its advantaged location at the edge of our solar system. This exciting discovery alone justified the expense and effort required to build the SIO on Sedna."

Dr. Vincent showed a slide of the observatory.

"The IWAU built their observatory inside the Gamma Crater on the hemisphere where our astronauts first landed. Neither the construction team nor the resident astronomers had the time or the inclination to explore the surface of Sedna outside of the Gamma Crater, nor has anyone done a systematic geological study of the planet's surface. Thus most of this dwarf planet including the obverse hemisphere remains unexplored and enigmatic."

The next holograph showed the obverse side of Sedna.

"Hired by the UWSF geological division, I have begun recruiting a team of eleven other scientists for a mission to explore Sedna's surface. Four other geologists, a mineralogist, an astrophysicist, an astronomer, two biologists, and a medical doctor have already agreed to join the Sedna geological exploration team. Our objective will be this side of Sedna. Because of the thirty-one-month journey to Sedna, a year at the SIO, and another thirty-one months to return, the mission requires a six-year commitment. I am now looking for a sixth geologist or mineralogist to join our team. If anyone is interested, please contact me."

Dr. Vincent finished his lecture with another challenge for a twelfth member of the team to join. During the lecture, an assistant handed Jerry a note from Dr. Vincent. He wanted to see Jerry in his office immediately after the lecture, and Jerry had a good idea what motivated this request.

Dr. Vincent did not waste time with preliminaries when Jerry entered his office.

"Have you considered joining our Sedna Geological Expedition team?"

Jerry did not immediately answer. Dr. Vincent ignored Jerry's silence and continued his pitch.

"I would like you to consider my offer. I need your expertise on the surface of that dwarf planet. This expedition will be a lifetime opportunity for each of us."

After the challenge that Dr. Vincent threw out during his lecture, his question and offer came at no surprise to Jerry who hesitated for a few seconds before answering.

"Yes, I have thought about it, but my family will find the idea of a six-year absence from them unacceptable. I just returned from a six-month meteor hunting expedition in Antarctica, and Carol wasn't happy about my absence during that relatively short mission. Aden is twelve years old, will be eighteen before my return, and will have grown into a young man. He needs a father during these formative years. I am excited about the offer, but I will have to talk to my family and sleep on it."

"I know that six years is a huge commitment, especially for a family man. A hundred years ago, such a journey to Sedna would have been impossible, for it would have taken over a decade with the available technology of that time. However, within the past thirty years, our improved technology has made such a journey possible. Our starship, UWSF Tesla, comes equipped with the latest fusion reactor and xenon ion generators. After a gravitational assist from Jupiter and Neptune, it will reach a peak speed of over 423,500 miles per hour, and 550,000 miles per hour on the return trip. Fast enough to get us to Sedna and back in five years with an extra one year stay on that minor planet.

"That I am even considering a six years absence will come at a shock to Carol and Aden. Nevertheless she Aden and I will have this discussion and I'll let you know our decision."

As soon as Jerry returned to his home in San Francisco, he told Carol about the offer from Dr. Vincent. As he expected, the idea brought tears to her eyes.

"Six years … you would be away for six years? How could you even consider such a long absence from your family? My God, Jerry, Aden will be eighteen when you return. He will not have a father to guide him through his formative years, and what am I to do without a husband for the next six years?"

Carol was even more upset than Jerry expected, so he thought it would be best to let the idea simmer for a few days. It was hard to argue against Carol's point. He wanted to accept Dr. Vincent's offer, but not without her approval.

"Let's both ponder it for a while."

The next day Jerry took Aden surf fishing for striped bass south of Fleishhacker's beach in San Francisco. The seagulls suggested that baitfish were running and the stripers wouldn't be far behind them. Aden waded into the surf and cast a lure beyond the first breaking wave. After a half dozen casts, he hooked onto a striper and line screamed from his reel. After fighting the fish for fifteen minutes, with the help of Jerry's gaff he landed the fish. They gave each other high fives. It was a beautiful 35-pound fish, and Aden couldn't have been more excited. Jerry took a picture of five-foot Aden holding his fish with the striper's head held just below his chin, its tail trailing on the ground. On their way home, Jerry told his son about the offer for him to go to Sedna.

"Where is Sedna?" Aden asked.

"It's is at the fringe of our solar system, much further away from the sun than even Pluto."

"How long will it take you to get there?"

"Over two and a half years."

"Wow. That's a long trip. How long will you be gone?"

"Six years."

"What does Mom think about all this?"

"The idea didn't exactly thrill her. What do you think?"

"Mom and I would be without you for six years. That's not cool."

"If I go you would be the man of the house. Can I depend on you to take care of Mom, and can I have your support should I decide to go?"

Aden thought the idea over for a few blocks, and then finally answered, "Yes."

"Let's not discuss this with Mom right now. I will bring it up again in a couple of days." Two days later, he broached the subject again with Carol.

Carol's eyes glistened with tears, but then she smiled and said, "It will be hard on Aden and I to be without you for six years, but this is an once-in-a-lifetime opportunity for you, and I know you really want to accept Dr. Vincent's offer. So call him and accept."

Jerry kissed Carol, thanked her for her support, and then called Dr. Vincent and accepted his offer.

"Next Tuesday we are going to have our first full team meeting," Dr. Vincent said, "and if you could attend, we will meet at 10:00 AM in the meeting room next to my office. I can then introduce you to the team and explain about our mission and travel plans to Sedna."

Jerry said he would attend, ended satellite phone call, and hugged Carol again.

"I guess we're committed," he said, tightening his hug.

****

Tuesday morning Jerry boarded the maglev train tube to LA from the terminus in downtown Fremont. The train made the 400-mile trip to downtown LA in just 55 minutes, and then the subway trip to Pasadena took a few minutes more. Jerry arrived at the meeting on time and Dr. Vincent took him from member to member beginning with Dr. Isake Mitera, the Caltech geologist and mineralogist whom Jerry had previously met in Dr. Vincent's office. Isake said the tests they ran on Jerry's meteorite confirmed Jerry's previous findings. "The sample indeed is older than our solar system and must have traveled here from another star system," Dr. Mitera reported.

Dr. Vincent next introduced Jerry to the team physician, Dr. Connie Jenkins MD, a dignified trim woman in her forties with auburn hair and sparkling hazel eyes. They exchanged pleasantries.

Standing next to Connie was Jerry's friend, Dr. Wendy Wilson. "You didn't tell me you were a part of this expedition when you suggested I take my meteorite to Caltech," Jerry said. "I bet you knew Dr. Vincent would make me an offer to join the Sedna geological team."

"Well, I am glad he did so," she said with a slight smile, "but I didn't know if he would make you an offer when we spoke in my office. Dr. Vincent talked me into joining his team after I called and told him about your meteorite."

Jerry then continued individually meeting each team member, shaking hands and exchanging a few words with everyone.

Jerry remembered previously meeting Dr. Saul Amos, a thirty-year-old geologist from the Colorado School of Mines, at a UWSF geological meeting a couple of years ago. They shook hands and Jerry mentioned their previous meeting. Saul seemed fidgety and eager to keep their introduction short.

Dr. John Edmund, a tall New Englander with an athletic build, was an MIT geologist from Boston who spent a year stationed on the UWSF Kepler Moon Base and published papers on lunar geology. Jerry said that he had read John's papers and complimented him about the careful research and thorough work.

Dr. Peter Ramos, a University of Illinois astrophysicist and cosmologist who, at sixty years old, was awarded a Nobel Prize for his work on gravitational waves and recently published a book on cosmology. He enthusiastically shook Jerry's hand. Despite his five-foot-five-inch height, Peter projected health and vitality as he smiled broadly at Jerry.

"It's good to have an astrophysicist with us," Jerry said.

"We'll have to have a discussion about cosmology," Peter answered.

"We'll have plenty of opportunity for that in the next six years," Jerry surmised.

Dr. Judy Stein, a slight middle-aged trim woman with long dark hair, was a geochemist from the Australian National University in Canberra and an expert in determining the age of rocks. As they exchanged handshakes, Judy smiled warmly at Jerry and mentioned that she had studied the age data of his meteorite and agreed that it was "older than dirt" and came from another star system. Her warm smile made his heart skip a beat.

Dr. Mary Atkins, who looked much younger than her forty-year career suggested, was a biologist from the University of Washington specializing in DNA analysis.

"I read your article about analysis of chromosomes, proteins, and certain metabolites in the September issue of *Scientific American*," Jerry said. "It was informative and well done." She thanked him for the compliment but her handshake seemed limp and hesitant.

Dr. Richard Cannel had recently joined the University of Washington Biology Lab and worked closely with Dr. Atkins. He had published two papers in biological journals describing the latest techniques for analyzing DNA samples. "I assume you and Mary are members of the team in the hopes we may find some biological evidence on Sedna," Jerry said.

"One never knows, "Richard quipped.

Lastly, Dr. Bill Summerset was a metallurgist from the University of Arizona where he managed the meteorite analysis laboratory at the university. The U of A housed the most extensive and complete meteorite collection in the world, including samples from Ceres, Mercury, and meteorites both found on Earth and those returned from expeditions to Mars and Pluto. Bill asked Jerry if he could examine the meteorite and perhaps even take it back with him to Arizona for further analysis. Jerry replied that he would be glad to lend it to him if he would agree to return the meteorite when he finished with it. Bill promised he would do so and send with it the resulting report.

Introductions aside, Dr. Vincent began to explain some of the details surrounding their voyage to Sedna on the Starship Tesla.

"The starship is in orbit around the moon, and it is from there that our journey will begin and end. We will gather at the International Space Station at Lompoc, California, on August 22 and board a shuttle for the nine-hour trip to the moon. After two weeks spent getting familiar with Tesla and preparing for the long journey, we will leave moon orbit on September 10, and a few months later, rendezvous with Jupiter for a gravitational assist. Then after another eleven months, we will rendezvous with Neptune for a second gravitational assist. Fifteen months after we leave Neptune, we will arrive at Sedna where we will stay at the Sedna International Observatory for nine months. When our rover is ready, we will begin our journey to the other side of the small planet. Our first exploratory journey across the surface of Sedna will last no more than a few days, and if all goes well we could schedule several more explorations over the next few months before we leave for home. One year after arriving on Sedna, the UWSF Tesla will leave orbit around

Sedna and return to the moon a little over six years after we left. Do you have any questions?" No one did, so Dr. Vincent ended the meeting trusting he would see them all again at the International Space Station.

Chapter Two
Starship TESLA

August 23, 2117

Jerry arrived at the Lompoc Space Station on August 22 and, after a brief orientation, boarded the Tesla shuttle with the rest of the team the following morning. Hours later Jerry watched from the shuttle observation window as they approached the Moon and slid into orbit around it. The moon looked so close that Jerry felt he could reach out and touch it. Mountains, craters, and mare drifted past as they caught up to the orbiting Starship Tesla, which even at this distance brightly gleamed in the sunlight.

Tesla was one of only two starships designed by the UWSF for deep space exploration. Tesla's sister ship, the Michelson, was dedicated to servicing the Lassell mining station on Triton and on occasion the Mars Transformation Project. Tesla had carried the first exploration team to Sedna in 2086, and later transported the construction team, materials, equipment, and astronomers to Sedna to build the Sedna International Observatory or SIO.

When the shuttle was only 100 meters away from the starship, Jerry commented to Dr. Connie Jenkins, who shared his window view, "The ship is absolutely beautiful ... she takes my breath away."

Connie smiled and replied with a slight sigh, "Yes ... that she does. They call it a starship and she is worthy of that label. A marvel of engineering that will be our home for five of the next six years."

The UWSF Starship Tesla, named after the twentieth century inventor, Nicola Tesla, included three distinct sections. The starship's shape reminded Jerry of a wasp, with a head and thorax connected to a bulbous abdomen by a narrow waist. In total, the ship was about 450 meters long from the head to the tapered abdomen. The egg-shaped head or Command Center was 80 meters long with a maximum width of 50 meters. The 250-meter long thorax or midsection was the living quarters and consisted of three discrete 150-meter diameter wheels each rotating in lockstep about a central hub. In the abdomen section connected to the thorax by a narrow open-girder waist or petiole was the Engine Compartment.

The head with two large "compound eye" windows and a gaping docking portal "mouth" heightened the wasp illusion. The shuttle maneuvered toward the "mouth" and with a gentle shudder attached itself to the air lock. After docking, the team members exited the shuttle air lock and gathered in the arrival portal while holding on to straps to avoid floating off. Captain Jack Ferguson, who introduced himself as the captain of the Tesla, was waiting for them and warmly welcomed Dr. Vincent and then shook hands with each team member.

"Welcome aboard Tesla, your new home for the next few years." Captain Ferguson then introduced them to Dr. Don Hitachi, the second officer and Tesla's chief engineer. Jack then pointed to a corridor that led into the interior of the ship.

"If you will follow Don to the auditorium, we will explain a little about this starship." Escorted by Don and another Tesla crewmember, they floated along the passageway that ran along the entire length of the central hub. Few on the team had ever experienced weightlessness before, and it was obvious from their awkward movements that it was going to take some adjustment for all to maneuver comfortably around this vessel. At a juncture marked "Deck Two" one by one they climbed into a six-foot wide tube that led to the outer portion of the second wheel module. As they floated along the access tube, the gravity provided by centrifugal force gradually increased until on exiting the tube, they felt the equivalent of half of the gravity they would feel back on Earth. Jerry commented that it was good to experience even this decreased gravity, as he felt disoriented while in free fall. When they all had climbed into Section Two, Captain Ferguson led the team along a wide corridor that circled the wheel and ended at the ship's auditorium. After they all took seats, Captain Ferguson introduced the team to Gina Tappan, Tesla's information officer.

Gina, a stately middle-aged officer with auburn hair pulled back in a bun, smiled and said it was a privilege to escort this geological team to Sedna. She mentioned that this would be her second round-trip onboard the Tesla to Sedna, having transported the SIO construction team and astronomers to that dwarf planet years earlier. As the room darkened, a laser projector displayed a holographic schematic of the ship's three sections.

"To produce gravity which is essential to maintaining your health, the three wheels or passenger sections slowly rotate about a central hub. The front section, central hub, waist, and engine sections do not rotate and you will have to get used to floating gravity-free when visiting those sections," Gina explained as she pointed to parts of the schematic that floated in midair immediately in front of her.

"The front section where you entered contains the docking and entry air lock, the command center, and viewing room. The midsection or passenger modules consists of three interconnected rotating wheels that we call decks. Each deck is autonomous and accessed through the central hub and access tube. The decks house the living compartments along the perimeter of each wheel," Gina detailed as she rotated the image and pointed to various sections with her hand.

"You have probably noticed there are no windows on these decks; there is a good reason for that. Space is a dangerous place for humans. Radiation from the sun and energetic particles from deep space continuously bombard Tesla. Earth has a natural magnetic shield that deflects most of these dangerous particles, so Tesla creates its own powerful magnetic shield that deflects most of those charged particles. Energetic neutrons and other uncharged particles that are too energetic to be deflected by the shield are absorbed by the outside portion of each deck, which contains a reservoir filled with tons of water. Water is an excellent absorber of space radiation, and it also functions as the water supply for the ship."

A second holograph depicted details of the midsection.

"The passenger modules or decks rotate around the fixed central hub about once every three minutes. The hub contains all the life support equipment and central passageway like the one you came through when you arrived. Everyone must access each deck separately through access tubes in the central passageway. As the three decks rotate about the hub, centrifugal force produces the effect of gravity necessary for your health over such a long trip. Positioned in the front of the ship are the air locks, the command center, and the viewing room. Only the decks rotate, so at first some of you may become disoriented while in free fall, but after a time you will get used to it and it will become second nature. Captain

Ferguson will take you on a tour of the Command Center and viewing room at the end of my tour. The first ring or 'Deck One' behind the front section contains staterooms, crew quarters, a kitchen, cafeteria, and a computer and library room where you can rest, study, or videophone your friends and family. 'Deck Two' features this auditorium, offices, a lecture hall, classrooms, a theater, and an entertainment room reminiscent of the 3D computer-generated hologram deck on the starship Enterprise depicted in twentieth century *Star Trek* programs. 'Deck Three' houses equipment rooms, a hydroponics room, machine and fabrication shops, storage lockers, and the recreation room that we will visit next.

"The aft section of Tesla houses the engines, a fusion reactor, electrical generators, and ion thrusters. It is connected to the midsection by an open girder 'waist' where fuels are stored in colored tanks."

Gina paused to ask if there were any questions.

Biologist Dr. Richard Cannel wanted to know more about the hydroponics room.

"In that room we grow most of the fresh food we will eat on this voyage. I can arrange for a tour of the garden tomorrow afternoon," Gina offered.

Dr. Peter Ramos asked if they were going to have a tour of the engine module before they left lunar orbit.

"Yes, I have arranged that tour for Tuesday morning. It will only be possible to do this before we activate the engines and leave lunar orbit on Thursday because of a small but unhealthy residual radiation. Those interested should meet with Dr. Hitachi here at 09:00 Tuesday morning."

Judy Stein wanted to know how many crewmembers were onboard.

"This will be the third voyage of Starship Tesla to Sedna, having made its maiden voyage over thirty-one years ago when it delivered the first exploratory team to that remote planet. Tesla is fully equipped for such long voyages. We have a team of eight officers who manage the starship, a crew of seventeen technicians, and a dozen androids that keep the ship running in top order. All our officers are graduates of the UWSF science academy and several have PhD degrees in astrophysics and space science. For many, this will be their second or third voyage on Tesla or on our sister Starship Michelson. Chief engineer Hitachi has been on each of the three previous Tesla voyages to Sedna. This will be my second voyage on Tesla. The crew has been trained to make you as comfortable as possible for the entire five-year duration of this mission. Trust that the crew has lots of experience ferrying passengers on long voyages in outer space. Our objective is to create an environment as close to that on Earth as possible. If there are no further questions, I'm sure you would like a tour of deck three."

The Sedna team members followed Gina down the central passageway tube leading to Deck Three and gathered in the recreation room. The high ceiling in the huge recreation room created the illusion of a blue sunlit sky that bathed the room in a warm glow. A slight breeze that smelled of the ocean caressed their cheeks. Exercise machines lined one side of the recreation room and in the center was a 5x10 meter swimming pool.

"The recreation room will be open 24/7. One of our staff, Jean Peters, is a certified trainer and she or one of her assistants will be on duty here at all hours. You can perform calisthenics, plan a workout, and swim in the warm pool or just lounge on a deck chair. You can hike along an enclosed corridor walkway that runs around the outside this deck and creates a computer-generated illusion of walking or jogging on an outdoor trail."

They looked inside the hydroponics room and noted the row of storage lockers before returning to the central hub. Several passengers complained that they felt dizzy and disoriented as the gravity decreased when they moved along the tube that led from deck three to the central passageway. Without gravity in the hub or access tubes, everyone had to grab handholds to pull him or herself along to reach the other decks or the Command Module.

"You will all grow accustomed to being weightless," Gina promised.

Dr. Connie Jenkins asked if she could visit the medical facilities.

"The clinic is with the main living quarters on Deck One," Gina said. "I will take you there after we visit the Command Center."

Wendy wanted to know without windows where they could view space outside the ship.

"One channel on the viewing screen in each bedroom provides a look forward and another aft." Then she quickly added that a viewing room in the front section next to the Command Center contained large video screens and that they would visit the viewing room after the Command Center tour.

Captain Ferguson again welcomed the team as each member entered the Command center. It was much smaller than Jerry had imagined. Command desks with individual computer screens lined both walls. Spanning the entire front of the command center was a large central window. The window looked real, but it wasn't. Rather than a real window, a 3D video screen spanned across the entire front of the module. The moon's surface drifted across the screen as the Tesla orbited above it. Captain Ferguson touched a switch and the view changed to that of the Earth, a blue soccer-size orb partially covered in white clouds with Asia and the South Pacific clearly recognizable.

Captain Ferguson explained the role of the various command desks around the outer wall of the center. Large flat screen instrument displays hovered above each desk, and airline buckle restraints kept each operator safely in their chair. The command posts included navigation, engine management, communications, and environmental control. Don Hitachi, the chief engineer, said he was eager to give them a tour of the engine section, but this would have to wait until Tuesday morning.

Their next visit was to the viewing room that included seating for a dozen folks. Designed for personal comfort, the room was small and intimate and included an automated refreshment counter that dispersed coffee, tea, and other refreshments in small bags with a tube to deliver the liquid into one's mouth. Two three-foot by two-foot windows provided a forward view from the comfortable lounging chairs with restraints. A twelve-inch reflecting telescope between the two windows delighted Wendy.

"What would you like to see next?" Gina asked.

"The entertainment room on Deck Two," Dana said without hesitation.

"Follow me to Deck Two then," Gina said.

Moving on through the access tubes to Deck Two, Gina led them into the entertainment room. The room, empty, measured eight meters wide, eight meters deep, and three meters high. A grid covered the blank white walls, floor, and ceiling. As a demonstration, Gina programmed a short travelogue of the Grand Canyon into the computer. Suddenly the team found themselves looking into the canyon from a glass observation platform suspended over the south face of the canyon. The holographic display was like the holodeck presentations on *Star Trek's Enterprise* and real enough to threaten Jerry with vertigo. Gina encouraged team members to walk around the deck where they could see magnificent views of the entire canyon. Jerry became queasy as he took a few hesitant steps out onto the platform and then quickly retreated inside.

In the next demonstration, Gina invited Dana to take a turn on a simulated flight into the canyon on a hang glider. She accepted the challenge and soon found herself flying dangerously close to a canyon wall. She gasped and her stomach dropped as the glider plummeted headlong into the abyss. She felt the wind rush against her face and experienced the smells and sounds of a real flight into the canyon. When the ride ended, Dana said that the ride was so realistic she became disoriented and dizzy as the canyon wall flashed bye with nothing but air between her and the canyon floor thousands of feet below.

Dana looked at Jerry and said, "Don't give the hang glider a try. If the observation platform scared you, the glider will make you airsick."

After an hour in the entertainment room and everyone had a chance to explore various demonstrations of their choosing, Gina gathered the passengers around her.

"This finishes our tour," she said. "I will take you to Deck One and escort you to your individually assigned staterooms. After a short rest in your stateroom, please meet me in the cafeteria located next to the staterooms at 06:00 for dinner." The individual staterooms were small but comfortable and included a bathroom, closet, and automated food dispenser. The utilitarian furnishings in Jerry's room consisted of a bed, an easy chair, a viewing screen, a table and chairs, and a writing desk with a personal computer and an overhead viewing screen. Jerry sat down in the lounge chair and turned on the 3D viewing screen. The same picture of the moon that he saw in the control center appeared. He pushed a button on the arm of the lounge chair and scanned through the list of available videos. He laughed, for one video was that of the century-old *Star Trek Next Generation* TV series. He selected it and watched for a while, amused at how similar the interior of the Tesla Command Center was to that of the starship Enterprise. Dinner that night consisted of pot roast and potatoes. Jerry ate dinner with Bill Summerset, Wendy, and Peter who commented that the food was well prepared and tasty.

Jerry and six other members of the team showed up at the appointed time on Tuesday for the tour of the engine module. Chief Engineer Don

Hitachi greeted them at the front of the petiole that led to the back sections of Tesla and provided a short introduction.

"As you know, this 7.5 billion mile trip to Sedna will take over three years. It takes that long because we will start rather slow and gradually build up to our maximum speed of over 400,000 miles per hour, but that speed will not be achieved until Tesla has traveled nearly halfway between Neptune and Sedna. We will begin and end our voyage using our VASMIR engine, which later on I will explain more fully. Tesla will spend most of the trip accelerated by our IONISTAR ion engine, to be switched on in a few days and remain so until we arrive near Sedna. With the assist of a fly-by of Jupiter and another by Neptune, after some months we will achieve our maximum speed and then rotate and use VASMIR to slow Tesla down for insertion into Sedna orbit."

He then led them into a transparent blue tube that ran the along the petiole to the front of the engine section. The petiole of interconnected steel girders that surrounded the tube and held seven tanks each individually painted red, green, blue, yellow, purple, and orange.

"The tanks provide the fuel and gases for our long trip to Sedna. The red tank contains argon for our magnetoplasma rocket, the green tank helium 3 for our fusion reactor, the large blue tank liquid oxygen, the yellow one liquid nitrogen, the purple tank holds liquid hydrogen, and the two orange tanks xenon for our plasma thrusters.

Peter Ramos noted the seven fuel tanks each seemed small for such a long trip.

"Is that enough fuel for a six-year journey through space?"

"Yes, it is more than enough for even a fifteen-year trip," Don clarified, "but we will renew our supply of water and fuel needed for the return trip home when we reach Sedna. One microliter of helium 3 in our fusion reactor can produce the energy equivalent to a 1,000 megawatt hydro-generator. Our thermionic generators when activated by the heat produced by our reactor will produce almost unlimited electrical energy to power the starship and the reactor containment field and plasma generator. The xenon supply is sufficient to drive the plasma engine for many years. There is only enough argon to initially accelerate Tesla and break our acceleration when we arrive close to Sedna. While you folks are on Sedna for a year, Tesla will remain in orbit and resupply for the return trip.

They entered the engine control room and gathered around Dr. Hitachi as he explained the function of the reactor, generators, and thrusters with schematics displayed on a 6x9 foot viewing screen.

"The engine section contains the fusion reactor, the electrical generators, the magnetic shield generator, the magnetoplasma engine, and the ion thrusters."

"The fusion reactor or Spheromak is a magnetic bottle designed to keep the fusion reaction away from contact with the sides of the container that would otherwise dampen the reaction. A charged plasma of helium 3 is RF heated to millions of degrees and then injected into the center of the Spheromak where additional heating and pressure fuses the helium 3 into helium 4, a free proton, and produces millions of ergs of energy. The protons are converted into electrical energy by a megawatt thermionic generator that provides direct power to the starship and produces the high voltage necessary to energize the Spheromak magnetic bottle and the magnetic field shield that protects us from high energy particles zooming around outer space. The electrical energy also powers the plasma engine VASMIR and ion engine IONISTAR."

Don pointed to the 6x2 foot closet-size black box depicted on the viewing screen.

"This is the magnetic field generator or MFG necessary to protect us from deadly Corona Mass Ejections, the solar wind, and interstellar cosmic rays that we will encounter during our long journey through space. The MFG creates a magnetic shield that deflects dangerous particles away from our starship. Without this magnetic shield, much of our DNA would be altered or destroyed during this long journey."

On the next two slides, Don explained how the engines that drive Tesla work.

"Besides the fusion reactor, Tesla has two different types of thruster engines: a magnetoplasma rocket known as a VASIMR, and an ion array thruster called IONISTAR.

The Variable Specific Impulse Magnetoplasma Rocket (VASIMR, for short) consists of three linked magnetic cells. The first stage works a bit like a kettle, heating the atoms of a neutral gas like argon with a radio frequency (RF) generator until electrons "boil" off, creating plasma. The plasma is very hot—about 50,000 degrees Celsius—but not hot enough to produce efficient thrust. The second stage of VASIMR acts as an amplifier and further energizes the plasma with electromagnetic waves. By now, the plasma has reached about a million degrees, comparable to the temperature in the sun's corona but millions of times denser than that gas. The third and final stage is a "magnetic nozzle" that converts the energy of this superheated plasma into a stream of particles that provides a high velocity but weak thrust. The plasma would melt any materials that it contacts, so it must be confined by a magnetic bottle."

"However, the VASIMR is only designed to provide the initial momentum for Tesla, about 2,500 newtons, enough thrust to break Tesla out of lunar obit and provide the initial velocity to send us on our way to a rendezvous with Jupiter. The VASMIR engine will also provide the necessary breaking for insertion into Sedna orbit. We will repeat the whole process for our return trip."

"Although thousands of times more powerful than the ion thruster, VASMIR has a limited supply of argon fuel and cannot operate continuously for more than a few weeks. For the balance of the voyage, we will depend on the constant thrust produced by the IONISTAR ion engine that over several months will speed up Tesla to its maximum outgoing velocity of 423,500 mph. VASMIR will again be switched on when we are three months away from Sedna, this time to slow Tesla down for insertion into Sedna orbit."

The view screen depicted a cutaway view of IONISTSTAR as Don continued.

"Ion thrusters work, as the name suggests, by firing ions (charged atoms or molecules) out of a nozzle at high speed. Xenon is squirted into a chamber and the electron gun fires electrons at the xenon atoms, creating a plasma of negative and positive ions. The positive ions diffuse to the back of the chamber, where high-charged accelerator grids grab the ions and propel them out of the engine, creating thrust. Protons released by the helium 3 fusion reaction are directed to the radioisotope thermoelectric generator that produces the high voltage necessary to power the electron gun. The thrust produced by each ion generator is feeble, only 250 newtons. However, Tesla has twenty-four ion generators arranged around the VASIMR port and, when continuously operated for about twenty-two months, and in combination with a boost from Jupiter and Neptune, will accelerate us to the maximum velocity between Neptune and Sedna.

"That is an impressive speed. Wouldn't this be enough to travel to another star system?" Connie Jenkins asked.

"However impressive our present technology may seem, it is not practical for an interstellar trip," Don replied. "Even with our advanced technology and achieving our peak speed, it will still take us twenty-five months to traverse the 7.5 billion miles from Earth to Sedna. The nearest star system that has a planet with an environment like Earth is seventeen light-years away, or almost 100 trillion miles. Even accelerating for months and achieving a top speed of over one million miles per hour, it would take Tesla over 28,000 years to reach it."

Don smiled at Connie. "Yet never say never. Our engineers and scientists are working on a direct drive fusion reactor that they say could power a starship up to 10 percent of the speed of light, or 67 million miles per hour. Yet even at that fantastic velocity, it would still take us over 200 years to reach that distant star system. This is why we have no evidence of an extraterrestrial visit. The journey is daunting for even the most advanced race.

Saul Amos softly whistled. "And that 200-year journey is just to get there, not to mention a return trip. So what practical use is there for a direct drive fusion reactor if it can never get us to another star system?"

"At a maximum velocity of 10 percent of the speed of light possible with a direct drive fusion reactor, this trip to Sedna would take only six months—three months accelerating and three months decelerating. A journey to our mining base on Triton with the direct drive fusion engine would only take four months. While Tesla can achieve impressive velocities, it can only achieve a fraction of the speed of light, and decelerating is as big a problem as accelerating. For instance, when we are three months away from our rendezvous with Sedna, we will rotate our Starship 180 degrees and activate the VASMIR engine to slow us down so we can safely insert Tesla into orbit around Sedna."

Don turned away from Saul and again addressed the entire group.

"Space is unfathomably vast. We marvel that we have established an observatory on distant Sedna, an unmatched achievement for human beings. Yet the nearest star is thousands of times more distant than Sedna—and yet no one can claim that we will never visit another star system. Our technology will continue to improve and perhaps someday interstellar travel will be possible by physics that we have yet to imagine.

Such physics remains in the distant future. Other civilizations somewhere out there may already have such technology, but if so, they don't seem to have made it here or perhaps they have no interest in us."

When the orientation ended, Don led the group into the heart of the engine module to view the fusion reactors VASMIR and IONISTAR close up.

"The helium 3 fusion reactor does not create the dangerous levels of radiation of fission reactors; nevertheless, there is enough secondary neutron and proton-induced radiation about that it is unsafe to visit here for very long."

The reactor was much smaller than Jerry imagined, only about the size of a large commercial refrigerator. Don opened a view port so they could see into the heart of the reactor. Even though the ultraviolet port made viewing possible and inhibited dangerous radiation, the plasma at the center of the magnetic bottle glowed with such an intense blue-white radiance that it was uncomfortably painful to look at it for more than a couple of seconds. Protons generated by the helium 3 fusion reactor activated six electrical generators located behind the reactor. Each generator consisted of hundreds of three by four foot electrical plates, and in total provided 1750 kW of direct current electrical power, enough to power the fusion reactor, the magnetic field generator, and the IONISTAR and VASMIR engines.

Behind the proton electrical generator, two transparent 500-gallon tanks of water used electrolysis to separate hydrogen and oxygen. Clouds of gas bubbles floated from the electrodes to the surface of each tank. The resulting gas is liquefied and then fed into pressure tanks located in the waist. The hydrogen thus produced powered a diffusion reactor located at the front of the engine compartment, which generated 250kw of ac power for Tesla. When combined with nitrogen from the tank in the waist, the oxygen produced in the tanks supplemented breathing air for the entire ship.

After the tour, the group returned to the passenger module cafeteria and met the rest of the geologic team who hadn't taken the tour. During lunch, Captain Ferguson announced that Tesla would activate its VASMIR engine tomorrow at 8:00 AM for a test before their scheduled departure to leave lunar orbit in transit to Jupiter.

"Perhaps some of you would like to observe that test," Captain Ferguson offered.

Watching the test didn't interest Jerry, and he thought the two weeks the passengers spent waiting for departure would bore him. He had a better idea how he might occupy that time. He contacted the Compton Moon Base and spoke with his colleague, Physicist and Geologist Dr. Matt Simpson, by videophone. As senior scientist, Matt had hired Jerry at UC Berkeley years ago and, during their time together, they had become good friends. After he retired from UC Berkeley, Matt worked on neutrino detectors and spent the past six years as the director of the Lunar Neutrino Telescope (LNT). The LNT was perhaps the largest and most complicated neutrino telescope ever constructed. Not only was Dr. Simpson the LNT director, he was also the foremost geologist and astrophysicist scientist in the UWSF organization and instrumental in getting the UWSF interested in funding the Sedna Geological Expedition (SGE). He also recommended his friend Dr. Josh Vincent to lead the SGE team. The Compton Moon Base or CMB was a small underground city designed to keep its citizens comfortable and productive. Constructed inside one of the large empty underground lava caverns that lie beneath the Compton Crater, the Lunar Neutrino Telescope resided twelve miles deeper under the CMB.

"Jerry, I would give my right arm to be going with you, John, and Josh to Sedna," Matt said. "This is the most exciting geological expedition in years. Nevertheless, my duties as the director of the LNT prevent me from joining the SGE expedition. I simply cannot afford to be gone for the next six years. I understand that John Edmund is also a member of your team. John spent two years with me at the Compton Moon Base helping determine the nature of the moon's subsurface, what causes Moonquakes, and characteristics of the moon's core. He has also authored several papers on the moon's origin from a planet collision with Earth. The data he collected was critical in selecting a proper location for the LNT. He is an excellent geologist and you are lucky to have him on your team. I wish you, John, and all of Josh's team the best of luck on Sedna."

Then Jerry made his request. "I understand that as Tesla prepares for our journey to Sedna it will be in lunar orbit for two more weeks," Jerry said. "I have never been on the moon. Is there any chance that I could visit the Compton Base and the LNT before we leave orbit?"

Matt smiled. "If you can catch a ride on one of your shuttles to the Compton Base, I would be glad to host you for a tour. Perhaps John and Josh would also like to join us."

"I will ask for permission for leave of Tesla and hitch a ride on the shuttle. I will also ask Josh and John if they want to join me."

There was no hesitation from either Josh or John when Jerry asked them if they wanted to visit the LNT. Even John, who had spent two long years at Compton, was eager to return. They both jumped at the chance to visit the Compton Base and the LNT. Jerry asked Captain Ferguson for permission for the three friends to ride the shuttle to Compton Base, and the captain said they could ride the shuttle on tomorrow's trip to the surface.

As the shuttle approached the moon's surface and flew over the Compton Crater, a large central dome and a smaller cubic building surround by three silos and acres of solar cells caught Jerry's attention.

"That is our helium 3 recovery factory," the shuttle pilot offered.

About a mile away from the dome was an open pit mine more than a mile in diameter. "They mine the lunar regolith that contains helium 3 from that pit," John explained.

Jerry commented that he could see no other evidence of man-made structures on the surface other than a hangar to which the shuttle flew.

"And you won't either," John said. "Most artificial structures on the moon are underground, except for the helium 3 factory we just flew over. Helium 3 is rare on Earth but abundant here in the Compton Crater. This industry supplies helium 3 for all the fusion reactors in the USA and indeed for Tesla's fusion reactor as well."

As they prepared to land, John explained further about the geology of the lunar surface. "In the twentieth century, geologists were confused about why the moon lacked theoretical density. Only after NASA explored the moon firsthand did they discover the moon's subsurface is like a piece of Swiss cheese, riddled with huge empty caverns. When the moon was geologically active, huge pockets of molten basalt formed underground and then when they erupted, the magma spewed out onto the surface and left behind these huge empty voids. The caverns provide a perfect place for the various moon settlements and science experiments, including the Compton Moon Base and the LNT."

The only structure other than the helium factory visible on the Compton crater surface was a large hangar near the northern rim of the crater. As they approached, the doors of the hangar opened wide and the shuttle landed inside. After the doors closed and the hangar repressurized, they disembarked and entered a large room that was both an airlock and an elevator. The Compton Base was a small city erected inside one of the large underground caverns, about 1,800 feet below the surface. It housed 1,300 scientists, engineers, technicians, and service and maintenance personnel. The elevator dropped so suddenly that Jerry's stomach felt like it was still on the lunar surface. When the doors finally opened and Jerry stepped out, the size of the city and immensity of the cavern amazed him. For over a quarter mile, buildings both big and small spread out in every direction, and over a hundred feet above the city the glowing cavern ceiling simulated a blue earthly sky. As soon as they had all exited the elevator, a jitney approached and stopped in front of them. Dr. Simpson jumped out of the jitney and after greeting Jerry, Josh, and John, warmly welcomed the other Tesla visitors.

Matt beamed. "Josh, it has been years since our last project together, and John, welcome back to Compton. It is so good to see you, folks. We don't get many visitors to the moon or at Compton."

Matt then loaded everyone onto the jitney and drove to a tall windowless building not far from the elevator. "Welcome to the administration offices of Compton," Matt said as he took them inside to a small auditorium where he could explain about the neutrino telescope.

"Neutrinos are small, almost massless, yet energetic subatomic particles thousands of times smaller than an electron. Because they have no charge and are almost massless they are extremely difficult to detect," Matt explained. They originate wherever a neutron decays into a proton and electron, like what happens inside the sun, particle accelerators, reactors, or out in deep space. Millions of them pass through your body every second without the slightest observable effect on you or on anything else. They can travel across the universe unaffected by their journey except by gravity. There are three types or neutrino "flavors" and they can change flavors in transit or oscillate between them. Our large LNT telescope can capture these infrequent collisions of neutrinos with matter, although we may see only one or two of these rare collisions each day. Yet even this paucity of data can tell us a lot about the early universe, star formation, supernovas, and gamma ray bursts. To avoid interfering radiation, the LNT is buried deep inside the moon, twelve miles below Compton. It consists of five billion gallons of heavy water, millions of detectors, and the largest quantum supercomputer ever built."

After the introduction, Matt took John, Dr. Vincent, and Jerry to another elevator. A sign above the elevator door read "Portal to the Home of the Little Neutral Ones," a play on Enrico Fermi's Italian name that he gave to neutrinos, Matt said.

The elevator operator instructed the passengers to stand against the back wall of the elevator and secured each one of them to the wall with harnesses. The reason for the harnesses soon became clear.

If Jerry thought the elevator trip to the Compton Base was stomach-churning, the trip on the LNT elevator produced a much more intense effect. Jerry became weightless as the elevator dropped into the twelve-mile deep shaft at a speed sufficient to overcome the moon's weak gravity. Then as they approached the end of the trip, the deceleration produced a force of 2g's on their bodies. Without the straps, each passenger would first float about the elevator and then be smashed against the floor as the elevator decelerated and came to a stop. It only took ten minutes to arrive at the bottom of the shaft, and Jerry was thankful when it finally came to that bone-jarring stop and the door opened. Feeling a bit woozy, he stumbled into a dimly lit corridor. Matt led the visitors to a brightly lit control room that reminded him of a reactor control room back on Earth. A dozen or more technicians and engineers stood in front of 3D touch screens that lined each wall. Occasionally one would reach inside the display to control various operations. Intent on monitoring their screens, they ignored Matt and his visitors. Matt then pointed to a large overhead screen that graphically displayed the results of the observations for the past week.

"Each line on this graph reconstructs a collision between an incoming neutrino and a heavy water deuterium atom. The lines show the direction, the thickness of the line the energy, and the color of the line the flavor of an individual incoming neutrino. As you can see, we have only detected six neutrinos in the past six days. While such collisions are rare, they tell us much about the universe and our sun."

"Why do some of the lines change color?" Josh asked.

"That's because the neutrinos often change flavor from electron to tau or to muon neutrinos in midflight. Tricky little devils these neutrinos are."

After a few minutes in the control room, Matt led them down a narrow hall to another room filled with long racks of equipment arrayed in twinkling blue, yellow, and red mini-lights.

Matt pointed to the racks. "This is our quantum supercomputer that integrates the results of the millions of detectors in the telescope and displays the data you observed on the overhead screen." Then he ushered them down another long narrow corridor that led to a huge observation window that looked onto what appeared to be a large swimming pool tank.

"This tank is one of 1,027 other cubic water tanks all arranged in a giant cube three miles on each side. The tanks are each filled with millions of gallons of purified heavy water, which thankfully is abundant in the surface ices of the Moon. The billions of incoming neutrinos that pass through the cube each second have a minuscule chance for just one of them to collide with one of these heavy water atoms, and when such a rare event happens, the collision provides a burst of gamma rays, occasionally a proton, or an electron that our detectors can measure. The chance of a neutrino colliding with a proton or neutron is like a bb colliding with a single tennis ball spaced ten miles from its nearest neighbor. There is a lot of empty space in substances."

"So what has the LNT told us about the universe?" John asked.

"The incoming neutrinos are unaffected by the space they traverse through and arrive at our telescope much as they formed some billions of years ago. Our sun releases theirs that take only minutes to arrive. From this data we have learned many details of the Big Bang and the formation and processes in stars and galaxies."

Matt then led them back to the elevator for the ride back to the Compton Base. The elevator's rise to the top of the shaft was more gradual than the decent and took twenty minutes so they didn't have to be strapped into the elevator. Back at the administration building, they enjoyed a dinner with Matt and his LNT staff before the ride back to the surface where their shuttle waited to take them back to Tesla.

Chapter Three
The Voyage

On Board Tesla, parked in Moon orbit September 10, 2117

Jerry, Peter Ramos, and Wendy Wilson made their way to the observation room at 7:30 AM to view the launch of their journey to Sedna. At exactly 8:00 AM, they could feel a gentle increase in g-force that indicated Tesla was accelerating. They watched as the moon slowly slipped away and, within the hour, the entire disk of moon had shrunk to the size of a beach ball. After a breakfast in the cafeteria, Wendy and Jerry returned to the observation room. By now the moon was a disk the size of a quarter and Jupiter, their intermediate destination, was visible on the forward screen as a brilliant light set in a vast field of thousands of stars. Three days later in what had become their daily visit to the observation room, Jerry and Wendy noted the velocity display now read 16,800 mph and was increasing at the rate of 5,600 mph every day.

One morning Gina Tappan, the ship's information officer, joined Jerry, Wendy, Mary, and Connie in the observation room, and Jerry mentioned to her that their speed was rapidly increasing.

"Twelve days from now Tesla will have reached a velocity of 85,300 mph and then we will switch VASMIR off to conserve our limited supply of argon," Gina said. "The IONISTAR engine will continue to accelerate Tesla toward Jupiter, yet at a much slower rate, adding only 330 mph per day to our starship's velocity. It will take us six months to arrive at Jupiter, yet by then IONISTAR will have speeded up Tesla to 143,800 mph. We will use that huge planet to slingshot us toward Neptune for another eleven-month journey and when we arrive at that gas giant our velocity will be 340,000 mph. Six months after our rendezvous with Neptune, we will achieve our maximum outgoing velocity of 423,500 mph, and then the problem becomes one of slowing down. Months before we are due to arrive at Sedna, Tesla will rotate 180 degrees and turn on VASMIR to decelerate us for insertion into Sedna orbit."

"Sounds complicated," Jerry commented. "I trust the ship's navigator knows what he is doing. After all Sedna is just a little planet, an insignificant rock in all this starry vastness."

Gina smiled and laid her hand on Jerry's shoulder. "It's not as complicated as it might sound. The quantum computer is our celestial navigator and the whole trip has been preprogrammed. Our navigator Dr. Marvin Thompson is just along for the ride, unless of course if something should go wrong, in which case he is a capable engineer and navigator."

"Of course, computers never experience problems," Wendy said sarcastically.

Gina smiled. "Even if our navigation computer decided to have a hiccup, Dr. Thompson can navigate us through space by the celestial navigation database stored in Tesla's computers. We are well prepared to navigate without that computer.

"How is the UWSF search for extraterrestrial life going?" Connie Jenkins asked.

"In the past 100 years," Gina answered, "the UWSF has visited almost every corner of our solar system and landed probes or humans on every planet, dwarf planet, moon, asteroid, and comet that is worth exploring. Yet other than evidence of some primitive life that evolved on Mars hundreds of millions of years ago, we have found no evidence of extraterrestrial life. Nevertheless, UWSF continues to explore and set up bases and the search for extraterrestrial life continues. Robotic machines have analyzed all the large gas planets and moons in the outer solar system and we work a mining operation on the surface of Neptune's large moon, Triton, and automated science stations on Pluto, Saturn's moons Titan and Enceladus and Jupiter's moon Ganymede. Six years ago, the UWSF sent a robotic lander to Jupiter's moon, Europa. Using a nuclear drill, the lander melted through 50 miles of ice and is now probing the interior of the salt ocean that lies beneath the ice-covered surface. So far, they have not discovered life but they are gathering a wealth of data. A science team is preparing for another expedition to Ganymede, the largest moon in our solar system. In fact, this Jupiter moon is larger than Mercury or Pluto and despite the failure of previous expeditions to find evidence of life in its subterranean oceans, the UWSF believes that another expedition with better equipment may be more productive. In the twenty-first century, probes determined that Ganymede has a core of molten iron, a magnetic field, and a rocky and thick icy surface and a subterranean ocean of salty water."

"Yes, the search for life is disappointing," added biologist Mary Atkins. "Other than on Earth and Mars, life just doesn't seem to have gotten a start elsewhere." "All the ingredients for life including amino acids and complex organic molecules exist in several extraterrestrial oceans, and even on comets and asteroids, but there is no evidence that those ingredients have gathered in liquid water to form life. I firmly believe that life is ubiquitous in the universe, yet the conditions are rare for life in this solar system."

As the weeks went by, Jerry and Wendy spent many afternoons together in the observation room, often alone. Jerry never tired of looking at the celestial view forward through the telescope. Jupiter now had a visible disk and he enjoyed the unimpeded rear view where Earth had shrunk to a blue ball the size of a marble and the sun the size of a nickel blazing off to the side. Now our moon was only the size of a BB-shot.

Two months later, as they crossed the orbit of Mars, the Earth was just a bright blue star. The closest they came to Mars was about 9 million miles, yet even at that distance, when viewed through the telescope the red planet was impressive.

Wendy explained that she had talked with the folks stationed on the Mars Terraforming Base (MTFB), which had been operational for over fifty-five years. Dozens of scientists and technicians lived in a large dome at the edge of the Bonestell Crater on Mars, the home of the Mars Terraforming Project. Each MTFP employee had committed to work on this project for three full years on Mars before his or her return to Earth.

The UWSF began the terraforming project in 2062 when they built the first factory at Bonestell, which processed Martian soil and released tons of carbon dioxide and nitrogen into the Martian atmosphere. They also melted the crater permafrost and filled it with water. Over the intervening years, the vast quantities of carbon dioxide released created a greenhouse effect that allowed global temperatures to rise above freezing for the first time in 500 million years. The project had filled the Bonestell Crater with a large lake and now subterranean ice all over the planet was melting and filling many other craters with melt water. After building more factories, the next phase of the project intended to introduce blue-green algae into the lakes, which would then release oxygen into the atmosphere. This phase of the project, expected to take at least another 125 years, would eventually transform the Martian atmosphere and temperature into a breathable environment that would allow humans to live and work on the planet's surface.

Entertainment on Tesla consisted of watching movies on in-room video systems, exercising or gaming in the recreational room, visits to the holographic room, or on special occasions lectures or events in the auditorium. The lectures presented by experts included subjects such as biology, physics, cosmology, and astronomy. A good example of these lectures was the one given by Dr. Peter Ramos, a renowned astrophysicist who had received a Nobel Prize for his work detecting gravitational waves. His other area of study was relativity, especially as it applied to time dilation. Dr. Ramon entitled his lecture, "On Time." Usually few passengers attended onboard lectures, but this one filled the auditorium. Dr. Ramos stepped to the podium precisely at 7:00 PM (on time), surveyed his audience, and began his talk.

"From Einstein's theories, we know that time is relative, yet I didn't expect so many folks would attend this esoteric lecture. The study of time is so counterintuitive that I fear that my lecture may only confuse some. If my talk seems to drag, that would demonstrate an aspect of psychological time uniquely experienced by each individual, but I hope this lecture will seem to fly by." Uncomfortable laughter spread throughout the room.

"To claim that time is relative or in the mind of the beholder was Einstein's attempt to explain his theory of relativity, which states there is no absolute time, as most of the nineteenth century scientists maintained. Time is unique to one's own location and time frame. The clock that ticks back on Earth does not tick at the same rate as it does for us here on Tesla."

Ramon wrote the time dilation equation on the whiteboard.

"As you can see, unless we were approaching close to the speed of light, the effect of time dilation is minimal. Even at over our maximum speed of 550,000 miles per hour (or over 100 miles per second), we will only be traveling at fewer than one ten-thousandth of the 186,000 miles per second speed of light, so our time dilation while onboard Tesla will be insignificant. Nevertheless, while the clocks on Tesla may run a bit slower than those back on Earth, the cumulative difference for us will amount to only a few minutes by the time we return home from this journey to Sedna and back."

Ramon went on to explain Einstein's theory of "block time," in which Albert claimed time is only an illusion.

"Einstein thought the past, present, and future is all the same, similar to taking a series of transparent movie frames and laying them on top of one another rather than projecting them sequentially. Fundamentally, I do not agree with the concept of block time. Time is a physical reality, and the proof is demonstrated at the quantum level where a subatomic particle will appear in different locations when observed at different instances. If time were only an illusion, it would be irrelevant to the particle's position. Time is real and has been marching forward since the Big Bang, yet it is not absolute. The universe has no master clock on which all observers can agree. Events occur sequentially at a rate unique to the time frame of the observer. Those observing from different time frames may not agree on sequences. Astronomers on Earth may announce that a supernova occurred last week in galaxy 20,000 light-years away, but it actually occurred 20,000 years ago not last week. Someone who lives in that galaxy may claim that it happened only 200 years ago."

Dr. Ramos recognized a raised hand in the audience.

"So, what you are saying is that Einstein was mistaken with his theory of block time, where he claims that time is only an illusion with no past or future, only the present."

"No, while I disagree with the concept of block time, I am saying that because of differing time frames there is no universal time on which all careful observes can agree. One of the anomalies of time is that observers may not even agree on the sequence of events. For example, nine and one half billion years ago a supernova exploded in a distant galaxy and the light from that explosion began its long trip to the Milky Way. Along the way, those photons entered a supergalaxy cluster where the gravitational curvature of space bent their path in such a way that they split into several identical impostor galaxies. One of those galaxies then passed through a super massive galaxy where extreme gravity slowed its transition time by several weeks. Recently, the light from the first groups of that ancient supernova arrived at the telescopes of our earthbound astronomers and lasted for a few days. Three weeks later the light from the second now delayed galaxy also arrived. Three weeks out of a journey that took over nine billion years isn't much of a delay, but it allowed astronomers to predict the delayed light from that explosion would arrive after the others and when it did as predicted, they were ready to capture the entire supernova explosion from its beginning to its end. We now have a record of the entire process of a supernova explosion. It was if they were able to look into the past and view an entire event as it happened. Truly astounding."

"So then, what exactly is time?" someone asked.

"Fundamentally time is a measure of change as measured by an observer. All matter in the universe that is above a temperature of absolute zero is subject to continuous motion and change. Molecules vibrate, iron rusts, planets rotate, suns explode, and unfortunately each of us age. While there is no such thing as absolute time, as a convenience we invented standard time measured with minutes, or seconds or Earth's yearly rotation about the sun to describe noted change. Some folks age more gracefully than others do and appear younger than their years suggest, but to avoid social blunders we measure relative time for them by their birth. Nevertheless, physical change is the real measure of time, not years. We place apples in cold storage to slow down the arrow of time to which they are subjected. A mammoth trapped in ice for 10,000 years ago may look as if it died a few weeks ago. All motion in a system ceases at absolute zero, including molecular motion. Molecules trapped in such a system are frozen in time. Relative time also progress forward dependent on framework factors such as a gravity or velocity which slows time down for the materials and creatures existing within those differing time frames."

Dr. Ramos concluded his lecture with some time dilation examples.

"All of our GPS satellites must make time dilation corrections for the relative frameworks. These time dilations occur because of the reduced gravity at their location in space and their velocity. More extreme examples can be cited such as those experienced by objects near a black hole or a starship traveling at close to the speed of light. Captive in our own time frame, it is impossible for observers on Earth to watch a black hole swallow anything. As the object approaches the black hole event horizon, we would watch the object slow down until it seemed to stop altogether. From our perspective that object will never reach the event horizon. However, for that object time would progress normally as the black hole swallowed it."

Dr. Ramos finished is lecture with, "Time is not an illusion, but a consequence of change that occurs at different rates depending on the time frame in which it exists. Nor is the measure of time absolute—it will give different results depending on the time frame of the observer. How counterintuitive is that?"

****

Five months after leaving the moon, their speed had increased to almost 143,800 mph and Jupiter grew to the size of a soccer ball. Four weeks later, it filled the observation window. When only a day away from the rendezvous with Jupiter, they passed close to Europa, whose ice-cracked surface reminded Jerry of a snapshot of Earth's North Pole icecap. Fascinated by their flyby of Europa, Mary Atkins, the team biologist, joined Jerry and Wendy in the observation room.

"The UWSF robot has melted a hole through fifty miles of ice to explore the vast European Ocean underneath," Wendy said. "Yet despite discovering all the organic chemicals necessary for life in that ocean, they haven't found any signs of life down there … at least not yet."

Jerry voiced his skepticism. "And there is a good reason for that. Liquid water and the proper mix of organic chemicals is not all that is required for life to evolve. While life can obtain energy from sources other than sunlight, in that deep ocean it will not receive the radiation necessary to modify DNA. Except for evidence of extinct microbe life found on Mars, biologists have only disappointment in their quest to find extraterrestrial life. UWSF established a research base on Titan back in the eighties, but they didn't find any signs of life on that frozen nitrogen and ethane orb or inside the little moon Enceladus where they thought its subsurface water ocean might harbor life, but it didn't. Just because Europa has an ocean does not mean it has evolved life."

"We will see," Mary said, sounding a bit offended. "There is a lot yet to learn in our solar system."

****

February 2118

The huge striped planet filled the observation as Tesla approached Jupiter. Mary commented that the yellow, red, and orange stripes made the planet look like a painted beach ball. Most of the passengers and crew crowded into the room for the 12-minute flyby as Tesla swung around Jupiter only 75,000 miles from the planet's upper cloud layers. They passed so close to the surface that it looked like they could reach out and touch the upper clouds. Over the past two hundred years, the giant red spot had shrunk to a quarter of the size it enjoyed in the twentieth century, yet all were impressed with the monster hurricane that could swallow Earth as Tesla silently passed over it. Several smaller white companion low-pressure regions accompanied the red spot, each one a large storm in its own right. Jerry watched the velocity display increase from 184,300 mph as they approached Jupiter to over 220,000 mph as they completed the flyby and headed toward Neptune.

Because Saturn and Uranus were on opposite sides of the Solar System and a respectable distance from their ship, each only presented only a small disk when Tesla crossed their respective orbits. Nevertheless, the observation room telescope provided spectacular views of those planets and their moons.

Days turned into weeks, and weeks into months as Tesla sped on to Neptune. The ION thruster added 330 mph each day to their speed and six months after the Jupiter flyby their speed had increased to 340,000 mph. As they brushed past Neptune, Dr. Josh Vincent and Mary Atkins joined Wendy and Jerry in the observation room to view the blue-green orb of Neptune that now dominated the observation window. White clouds circled the otherwise bland surface of the planet as the 16-hour rotation created winds that drove those clouds at over 400 miles per hour.

A more interesting sight was the moon Triton. As they arrived close to Neptune, they passed over Triton's surface at only 7,000 miles, which offered an extraordinary view of a moon slightly larger than Pluto is. The pink ice surface mottled by tectonic forces reminded one of a tortured cantaloupe and only a few craters or other major surface features marred the otherwise smooth plains. The frozen nitrogen and water ice surface glistened in the diminished sunlight, and a tenuous nitrogen atmosphere hung over the limb of the moon.

Wendy had studied this moon as part of her research and offered some facts as they flew by.

"Triton is a twin of Pluto and slightly larger than that dwarf planet. It is the only moon in the solar system that follows a retrograde orbit, which proves that it could not have formed around Neptune. Neptune probably captured it from the Kuiper Belt, its most likely birthplace, but to this day the origin and method of capture of Triton remains an enigma. It is one of the few moons that exhibits cryovolasim or ice volcanoes, and is the coldest body in the solar system, just a few degrees above absolute zero. The UWSF landed a geological team on the moon twenty years ago with the mission to explore the surface for valuable minerals. The moon's mostly craterless surface is comprised of metallic rock and water ice smoothed over by internal eruptions of water and nitrogen ice. Several large ice volcanoes powered by Neptune's tidal action constantly resurfaces parts of the glaciated surface. The moon's outer layers are also rich in many mineral resources, including deposits of most elements found in the periodic table. A few years ago, the UWSF established a research and mining base on the side of Triton that permanently faces Neptune and named their settlement the Lassell Station, after William Lassell who discovered Neptune's largest moon. The interior has a core of liquid iron and magnesium that after millions of years should have cooled, yet remains liquid, probably heated by internal radioactivity and tidal action with Neptune. This explains the moon's unusual density, magnetic field, and its subsurface ocean of liquid water and hydrocarbons."

As they flew over Triton, Jerry and Dr. Vincent contacted Dr. Ed Mackey, the director of the Lassell Station. They exchanged greetings and Dr. Mackey explained about the success of their mining exploration and recent mining efforts on Triton.

"This moon is a treasure trove of minerals," Dr. Mackey beamed. "We have found almost every element on the periodic table, including many rare earths. Our mining undertaking at Lassell produces many elements that are extremely rare on Earth. The starship Michelson, Tesla's sister ship, visits here every four years to deliver supplies and take our processed materials back to Earth. It is due to return next year. I wish you well in your geological expedition to Sedna."

As Tesla flew past Neptune, the velocity indicator increased from 340,000 to 374,000 miles per hour. The ion thruster would add another 330 mph each day until they achieved their maximum speed on the way to Sedna.

"We are now only fourteen months away from Sedna," Dr. Vincent announced. "In six months we will reach our peak velocity of over 423,500 mph, and then we have to rotate Tesla 180 degrees and use VASMIR to begin decelerating or at this speed we would fly right past Sedna."

After the Neptune flyby, they entered the trans-Neptunian (or TN) region of the outer solar system named the Kuiper Belt, where thousands of icy rocks and dwarf planets orbit the sun in century-long paths. Pluto, first visited over a hundred years earlier by the New Horizons spacecraft, is the most interesting of these TN objects. In the fifty years following the New Horizons flyby, Pluto became a major project for UWSF. Intrigued by the many surprises discovered by New Horizons, NASA and then UWSF sent several robots and then in 2056, a human team to explore its ice-covered surface, enigmatic mountains, and wispy ephemeral atmosphere. As Tesla crossed Pluto's orbit some distance from the dwarf planet, it presented a dime-size disk in the window with its moon Charon glowing against the vast tapestry of surrounding stars. In Tesla's observation room telescope, Pluto displayed a varied surface with high mountains, large plains, long deep scars, and yawning valleys. The pink "heart" first viewed by New Horizons was clearly visible. Tidal action from Charon caused Pluto's crust to flex, and internal radioactive decay kept the core plastic and thrust mountains and ridges of rock and ice thousands of feet above the surface. The weak sun's rays and constant tidal action raised the surface temperature enough at perihelion to provide a thin atmosphere of methane, nitrogen, and carbon dioxide. There had been a proposal within UWSF to place a base on Pluto, but the Sedna observatory and the mining base on Triton severely limited available funds. New Horizons also flew by the dwarf planet Eris in 2028. Almost as large and twice as far away from the sun as Pluto, Eris was only visible from Tesla as a bright "star." Other Kuiper Belt minor planets like Makemake, Haumea, Quaoar, and the planet Leto remained remote and unexplored as they drifted in the Kuiper Belt.

From Pluto's orbit, Sedna appeared as a mere sixth magnitude star. When astronomers first discovered Sedna early in the twenty-first century, although it was much smaller and more distant than either Pluto or Eris, it became obvious that this icy rock differed from other Kuiper Belt objects. Because of its tremendous distance from Earth and the ensuing long travel time, the Foundation sent only two robots to land there and limited their sojourns to only one hemisphere. Humans first set foot on its surface in 2086 and limited their exploration to a 50km-wide region. UWSF's interest in Sedna eventually grew and, because of its position at the very edge of the solar system, the agency swiftly moved to devote limited resources to building an observatory on this strange, remote dwarf planet. They erected an observatory in the Gamma Crater where the first explorers landed. The astronomers who operated the observatory showed little interest in geology or exploration of the opposite hemisphere and, as a result, the many mysteries on Sedna remained unsolved. The Foundation recruited Dr. Vincent to lead a team to Sedna and explore the geology of the planet.

Over the ensuing months, Jerry and Wendy continued to spend time together in the observation room, becoming less interested in exploring the solar system and more interested in exploring each other. They held hands and reminisced about their college years tryst.

Jerry missed his family. Since leaving the moon, communication with them had become increasingly difficult. As they crossed the orbit of Mars, it took over fifteen minutes to send a message and another fifteen minutes to receive a reply. As they passed the orbit of Saturn, it was only practical to record and receive prerecorded videos, which didn't satisfy Jerry's need for closeness. Beyond Neptune, the time lag was over four hours, and when they reached Sedna, transit time would increase to over eight hours. Twice each week Jerry recorded a video and transmitted it to Carol and Aden, and they in turn replied hours or days later. This form of delayed communication did not ease Jerry's growing feelings of loneliness and detachment from his family. He longed for intimate human contact, and his time with Wendy filled a void that had become abjectly painful. Their handholding in the observation room progressed to an occasional hug, then a prolonged kiss, and eventually some time alone together in Wendy's quarters. They discovered a storage room next to the central access tube that provided discreet privacy. Intercourse in the gravity-free environment of the storage room was a unique experience that satisfied them physically and emotionally. Jerry felt no remorse for his betrayal of Carol. Six years was a long time to be away, and Carol would understand that such temptations were unavoidable. For the two Tesla lovers, it seemed not so much an indiscretion as a means to fulfill a growing physical and psychological need. Jerry convinced himself that Carol would indeed accept and eventually forgive his transgressions.

Twelve months after the Neptune flyby, Sedna presented a dime-size disk to naked eye viewers and two weeks from their rendezvous, Sedna had grown to the size of a melon. Jerry and Carol watched the planet transition through the short Sedna day and night, which provided the opportunity to view both hemispheres. As they flew over the first hemisphere, the surface reminded them of the near side of our moon—dull gray, flat, and marked by hundreds of craters. Clearly visible was the largest crater on the planet, Gamma Crater, 1,730 meters in diameter and home to the Sedna International Observatory (SIO). The other hemisphere looked like it belonged to a different planet.

"The surface of the obverse hemisphere is a contrast from the SIO side of the planet," Jerry commented as they flew over the other side. "The vast plains on this hemisphere are as rusty-red as the surface of Mars and are pockmarked with depressions interrupted by small hills. Unlike the SIO side, this side has only a few craters." The most obvious feature was two parallel mountain ranges with a narrow valley sandwiched between them.

"I can hardly wait to explore the obverse side and the mountain ranges and narrow valley that separate the two hemispheres," Wendy said.

Chapter Four
Arrival on Sedna

March 23, 2120

After thirty-one months in transit, Tesla assumed an equatorial orbit around Sedna. The geological team viewed both sides of the planet in detail, which allowed them to select a route for the first surface expedition. As Dr. Vincent had depicted in his previous Sedna presentation, the most interesting planetary feature was the two parallel north-to-south mountain ridges separated by a narrow valley, which traversed the planet from pole to pole, splitting the planet into two distinct and disparate hemispheres. A week later, Dr. Vincent and his entire geological and scientific team boarded a shuttle and landed in Sedna's Gamma Crater, the home of the SIO. Dr. Pinot, the director of the SIO, and his management team warmly greeted them when they exited the hangar and air lock. The team spent the next few days touring the SIO and getting used to their new accommodations. They inquired how long it would be before they could begin their sojourn across the surface to the other hemisphere. The news was not good: it was going to take at least a month for the SIO mechanics and technicians to assemble and test the three rovers delivered from Tesla.

Three weeks later the team impatiently waited for the mechanics to complete assembly of the first two rovers. The long wait for the geological expedition to get underway was beginning to get on team member nerves, and many were restless and irritable.

Jerry gazed out the observation window of the Sedna International Observatory (SIO) cafeteria and scanned the star filled velvet sky and the Gamma Crater rim for the first signs of the bright star that would soon rise over the rim of the crater and mark dawn on this frozen dwarf planet. The anticipated sunrise would take less than a minute or two, but this sunrise marked a special day.

Sedna rotated in just over ten hours so each night or day on this world lasted only five hours, and Jerry had witnessed several sunrises on Sedna. Yet this one was special, for it marked daybreak of the day the expedition would get underway. His mood brightened as the sun, at this distance reduced to a brilliant white star, appeared over the rim of the Gamma Crater and leisurely rose over the frozen cliffs of the eastern crater rim. This little world, twice as distant from Earth as Pluto is, received feeble radiation from a sun too far away to present a visible disk. Yet as it rose, it cast faint shadows across the frozen crater floor. During the over two-and-a-half-year journey to Sedna, Jerry studied everything known to science about this little world. The few facts that astronomers had discerned about the geology of Sedna produced more questions than answers. He pondered those few facts as he continued to stare out the window and trusted that the expedition he had committed six years of his life to would answer those questions.

Jerry turned his attention to the Gamma Crater landscape. In the weak sunlight, the rock-strewn floor of the Gamma Crater appeared colorless, bland, and featureless, offering little to attract his attention. The one-third of a mile-wide Gamma Crater was the largest crater on Sedna and because of its flat, smooth floor and unobstructed view of the sky, the (IAU) had selected this crater to build the Sedna International Observatory. The objective of this distant viewing post was to explore the Kuiper Belt and deep space unhindered by solar glare. Predominantly littered with icy rocks and dwarf planets, astronomers suspected the Kuiper belt hid other sizable dwarf planets like Pluto or Eris. Some of these dwarf planets circled the sun in elongated orbits with their aphelia all pointing in the same direction, indicative there was some yet undiscovered object out there called Planet X that gravitationally influenced those orbits. Every 26 million years Earth suffers a barrage of comets that caused major extinctions. A companion to our sun with a 26 million-year orbit could be responsible for disrupting the cloud of comets in the Oort Cloud, and an observatory on Sedna might just confirm the presence of this illusive companion.

The unremarkable view from the window intensified Jerry's homesickness. This remote planet was cold, dark, and inhospitable. Such adverse conditions made him miss the warmth and brilliance of the sun almost as much as he missed his family and his colorful San Francisco home of brown hills, purple ice plant flowers, green grass, and blue sky. When viewed from Earth through a powerful telescope, one hemisphere of Sedna (aka 2003 VB12) appeared as red as Mars, but in this feeble sunlight, the crater floor displayed only shades of gray. He reminisced about his last time at home in San Francisco and the warmth of his family. In his mind's eye, his wife and son were fading memories, difficult to remember without looking at his wallet pictures or watching the videos that Carol sent weekly. It took so long (10.8 hours) for a message to travel the 7.25 billion miles from Sedna to Earth that real-time communication with Earth was impossible, so all the citizens of Sedna could do was to send and receive prerecorded videos from their friends and family. The last time Jerry and Carol traded videos, she reiterated how she had never been keen about his job with the IAU. Stationed at the IAU Observatory on the South Pole for three months every fourth year, he had only recently returned from the last deployment when the offer for a six-year mission to Sedna piqued his interest. Carol wasn't happy but accepted Jerry's commitment to another long mission.

Depressed, Jerry turned away from the window and joined Josh and five other geological team members who were enjoying breakfast at a cafeteria table. He sat down with them and poured himself a cup of coffee.

"It's a new day and sunrise on Sedna," he said with more enthusiasm than the event deserved.

"Really, so what is so special about a sunrise on this planet? It's still damned dark outside," geologist John Edmund complained. "I spent two years at the science station at the South Pole in Antarctica and never adjusted to the months of darkness I had to endure, and now we won't experience the light and warmth of our sun for years. It's depressing and a bummer."

Jerry winced at John's remarks. "Daybreak may not be a major event on this hunk of frozen rock, but it signals the day the mechanics promised to have completed the assembly and testing of our new rovers."

Josh smiled and put down his cup of coffee. "Well, I have some good news: the first rover is almost ready to go, but the second one will take another week before it is ready. If we want to risk it and leave on only one rover, we could be on our way just before the next Sedna sunrise. The plan is to venture out beyond the confines of Gamma Crater, cross the Metros Plain and surmount the Walnut Ridges, and complete our mission by crossing the Bandar Quarter, thus completing a first circumnavigation of Sedna."

Everyone at the table gave a "thumbs up" for the dangerous plan to circumnavigate Sedna using only one rover.

"It's about time that geologists got a chance to explore this rock, and I for one am tired of waiting to do so," Isake Mitera said, ignoring the danger imposed by traveling with only one rover.

Josh looked at Isake and then added, "Over the past ten years, the construction crews and astronomers on Sedna worked hard to assemble and operate the SIO, yet they showed little interest in, and learned virtually nothing about, the geology or composition of Sedna's surface. That wasn't their mission. The few robotic rovers they deployed only explored this crater and the immediate vicinity beyond it. With our long-distance rovers, we will be the first humans to venture beyond the crater rim, explore Sedna, and travel to the mysterious red hemisphere."

Dr. Vincent took another sip of coffee. "I have finalized the plans for our first mission with the UWSF managers. We will travel 100 km east to the edge of the Walnut Mountains, cross over those two ranges, and then explore the geology of the opposite side of Sedna then return to the SIO."

Peter Ramos, the team's only astrophysicist, chimed in. "What fascinates me is the two opposite faces of Sedna, each so different from one another. It is as if a different process formed the two hemispheres."

Judy Stein interjected, "I think that could be true. The parallel mountain ridges that separate the two hemispheres indicates the planet formed from two separate bodies that smashed together in the distant past. When viewed some distance away, Sedna reminds one of a walnut, and inspired astronomers to name the ridges the Walnut Mountains."

Peter smiled at Judy and resumed. "Even with our most powerful space and moon-based telescopes, astronomers couldn't solve the many mysteries that surround this dwarf planet. Something seems very strange and foreign about this icy rock, especially regarding the different composition of each hemisphere, its high density, and elongated orbit. Our mission is to solve the mysteries of the origin and composition of this planet."

"Dwarf planet," Planetary astronomer Dr. Wendy Wilson corrected.

"All right, Wendy, I stand corrected." "The proper label is a dwarf planet," Peter said reluctantly. "Nevertheless, I never liked demoting Pluto from the list of planets in the first place, but since Sedna is less than half of Pluto's diameter, it truly is a dwarf. Yet Sedna's small size does not lessen its scientific charisma or importance. To my way of thinking, Sedna is just a small planet."

"Please excuse my insistence," Wendy said rather defensively. "It's important to recognize demoting Pluto from the list of planets was entirely necessary. When astronomers discovered Eris in the Kuiper Belt and found that it is almost as large as Pluto is, they initially called it the tenth planet. Then astronomers discovered dozens of other trans-Neptunian objects or TNOs, many smaller than Pluto and a few like Eris have diameters that rival Pluto's. Faced with a growing number of planets, some even with their own moons, the International Astronomical Union faced a dilemma. Did we have nine, ten, or dozens of planets? If Pluto is a planet, why exclude Eris, Makemake, Quaoar, and Haumea? The IAU solution was to demote Pluto and its TNO family to minor or dwarf planet status and admit the solar system contained only eight planets. Astronomers classified other natural objects, the majority smaller than our own moon and a few larger ones like Titan, Triton and Ganymede, as moons if they orbited a planet, or if they orbited the sun, as an asteroid, a comet, or a dwarf planet like Ceres. Sedna orbits the sun and, despite its small size, it is as dense as Mars. For this and other reasons, this dwarf planet deserved UWSF attention."

"You're both forgetting about the recently discovered TNO Leto," Jerry said. "With a diameter of 3,100 miles this TNO is larger than either Pluto or Mercury, but because of its average distance from the sun of 85AU, traveling in an orbit outside the solar plane, and sporting an albedo similar to that of coal, it went undiscovered until 2196. Leto added fuel to the entire planet classification controversy. If this huge TNO, which like Nemesis may affect the orbits of Eris and Haumea isn't a planet, then Mercury shouldn't be classified as a planet either."

"Perhaps planets should be classified based on some arbitrary diameter such as 1,400 miles. This would classify Pluto, Eris, and Leto as planets," Dr. Vincent suggested in an attempt to mediate.

"So if we set that arbitrary diameter to 900 kilometers, then Sedna which has a diameter of about 955 kilometers is a planet," John argued.

"Yes, but whether classified as a planet or dwarf planet most astronomers believe that Sedna doesn't belong to our solar system and shouldn't be here in the first place," Judy added as she nodded at John. "They claim it formed around some other star, perhaps Nemesis, and then millions of years later our sun kidnapped it on a close approach. That could explain its weird elliptical orbit outside the plane of the solar system and might also explain its red color and unusual density."

"That is exactly why we are here," Dr. Vincent reminded them, "to explore and better understand this alien world. Perhaps those astronomers who lived in the alien star system where Sedna may have been born considered it a planet, assuming such folks existed millions of years ago."

Josh filled his cup with a second helping of coffee and continued. "Of greater interest is that we have decided on our first expedition route and scheduled the ten-day mission to circumnavigate Sedna. Our first objective is the valley formed by the Walnut Mountains that we will explore during the faint daylight offered by the distant sun. After exploring the valley, we will cross over the eastern ridge and head across the Bandar Quarter, arriving back at the SIO after completing the first circumnavigation of Sedna."

Josh finished his coffee and concluded, "Just before the next Sedna sunrise a few hours from now, we will meet in the transport room and prepare for our departure in one of two rovers. I trust you are as excited about this as I am."

Everyone nodded, expecting that their journey was finally about to get underway.

Jerry excused himself, and went back to the observation window. The sun had moved a hands width from its position above the crater rim. The meager sunlight had brightened the crater floor, creating long shadows from the many boulders strewn about. "It will be another five hours until it sets again, and another sunrise will soon follow," he pondered. "It is hard to get used to a five hour day and night cycle."

Jerry returned to his quarters and, after listening again to Carol's last message he received over a week ago, his homesickness deepened. He felt guilty for not having responded in a more timely fashion to her last message, and began to feel guilty about all those afternoons he spent alone with Wendy. He recorded a long, news-filled answer that focused on his excitement about tomorrow's journey and tried not to betray his homesickness.

Six hours later Jerry joined Dr. Vincent and the rest of the twelve Sedna scientists who had gathered outside the rover in the SIO hangar. Peter Ramos, the team astrophysicist who Josh had assigned to be the rover driver, was already inside the rover examining the controls and running through a checklist. Those gathered around Josh at the steps of the rover included Wendy, John Edmund, Saul Amos, and Isake Mitera. As Jerry approached the group, he and Wendy exchanged smiles. Judy and Bill Summerset the team mineralogist were quietly talking at the front of the rover with biologists Mary Atkins and Richard Cannel. Physician Dr. Connie Jenkins was inside the rover checking her medical supplies. Dr. Vincent called for everyone to gather around him, and in the glare of the bright garage lights he offered a few final words before departure.

"The sun will set in another six hours. The paltry light offered by the distant sun isn't much, but it is far better than total darkness. Therefore, we will do most of our exploration during the short Sedna day. We will leave as soon as the rover is ready." He ended with a short prayer asking for God's blessing.

****

May 2, 2120

Mechanics were going over last-minute checklists for the yellow-painted rover that Dr. Vincent had named Sally, after his wife. Fully equipped with eating and sleeping accommodations for the team, Sally came filled with every analytical instrument that any university science lab would be proud to own. Mechanics checked the nuclear generator, verified that the batteries were fully charged, tested communications, booted computers, and activated other instruments and electronics essential to a successful mission. They gave special attention to the environmental systems, especially the oxygen generator, CO_2 scrubbers, and the pressure and temperature controls.

The plan was to drive Sally out of the crater across the 100 km-wide Metros Plain collecting samples along the way before surmounting the western Walnut ridge. The next day they would drop down into the valley between the western and eastern ranges, collect and analyze samples, and record geological data. After two days in the valley drilling exploratory holes and conducting seismic experiments to hunt for subsurface water, they would surmount the eastern Walnut ridge and take three days to cross over the Bandar Quarter and then return to the SIO. The mission would take five days and cover 4,000 km.

"Time to suit up," Josh instructed his team.

Twenty-second century space suits were different from those bulky outfits that hampered spacewalkers in the late twentieth century. These fabrics were light, tough, flexible, and comfortable. If necessary, the team members could wear them without discomfort for several days. They dressed in the protective suits and then scrambled into Sally as everyone else in the hangar retreated into the safety of the airtight inner building. After the hangar was depressurized, the outer air lock door opened and Peter Ramos carefully drove Sally out onto the floor of the Gamma Crater. It was difficult to make out anything beyond the light beams from Sally's headlights, but to Peter the crater floor looked flat and featureless. As they drove east toward the crater rim, the crater bluffs finally appeared in Sally's headlights

"Although the cliff is only 200 meters high, the approach is steep, so I'm going to look for a low pass where we can more easily exit the crater," Peter told them.

As the sun peeked over the crater rim, he drove Sally around the crater floor perimeter until he found a gap in the cliff. The traction offered by the six-drive wheels on Sally easily carried them up to the rim of the crater, where they stopped to survey the Metros Plain. Illuminated by the sparse light provided by the sun and overhead stars, the terrain below reminded Jerry of the surface of the Arizona desert at twilight— drab, flat, and featureless. Visible in the distance, the Walnut Mountain ridges 100 km away took on a red cast.

"They look a lot taller than 1200 meters," John Edmond commented about the ridges.

"Our challenge is how to find a way over or around them," Peter responded. He scanned the mountains with imaging binoculars, but from this distance he couldn't locate a gap or an obvious pass.

They deployed a repeater on the crater rim to enable communications with the SIO, but in the deep penetrating cold it wouldn't turn on.

"Perhaps after the internal heaters warm the electronics the transmitter will automatically turn on," Saul explained.

"Let's hope so," Dr. Vincent said. "After we are on the Metros Plain it is important to keep in contact with the SIO."

"Once over the mountains we will probably lose contact anyway," Peter said.

"Not necessarily. We'll place another repeater on top of the Walnut Ridge which should allow us to keep in contact the SIO, that is if the Gamma repeater will turn on," Josh said.

Sally moved down the crater rim and drove across the flat Metros Plain pockmarked here and there by small craters. The outside temperature indicator read minus 260 degrees centigrade, the magnetic field indicator recorded 0.55 gauss (about ½ that of Earth's magnetic field), and gravity was 0.33 g, or a third of that on Earth.

"I'm blown away by these gravity and magnetic readings on the Metros Plain," Judy commented. "It is hard to explain such large gravity and magnetic readings from such a small planet." The gravity readings should only be 0.15 g or so considering Sedna's diameter, and the magnetic field readings on Metros are much stronger than the readings we took in the Gamma Crater."

Saul Amos explained, "Sedna at 6,200 kg/m^2 has the highest density of any planet or dwarf planet in the solar system, which would account for the large gravitational reading. We knew that Sedna had a weak magnetic field but this strong field is more than I expected and much higher than inside the Gamma Crater."

"These anomalies are what we are here to try to explain," Dr. Vincent said.

Avoiding the occasional crater, Peter drove Sally along the featureless surface at thirty-five kilometers per hour. Jerry noticed in the glare of their headlights that the dust raised from Sally's wheels fell to the ground in gentle swirls, signaling the presence of a tenuous atmosphere, perhaps a meter or two thick. He mentioned this to Judy Stein.

"This is summer on Sedna as it retreats from perihelion, and our sun provides sufficient radiation to raise the surface temperature enough to sublimate nitrogen and methane" she replied. "Even at 77AU from the sun, we can expect a thin but tenuous atmosphere."

"Perhaps we should stop and capture a sample of the surface soil and atmosphere?" Josh suggested.

Peter brought Sally to a stop and Jerry and Josh prepared for an extravehicular sojourn on the Metros Plain. They donned boots, gloves, transparent bubble headgear, and a bulky backpack that provided protection from the near-vacuum on Sedna and from the deep cold of the planet's surface. Ten seconds exposed on this surface without adequate protection would result in a quick and gruesome death. The backpacks contained oxygen tanks, rebreathers, and power sufficient for a ten-hour odyssey outside the rover, but because of the low gravity on Sedna, the backpacks weighed only twelve pounds.

Dr. Vincent depressurized the rover's air lock and Jerry stepped outside for his first walk on the surface of Sedna. Peter turned off Sally's headlights and from where they had parked, the sun cast a shadow from the rim of the Gamma Crater. The sudden inky blackness and awareness of near-absolute zero temperature shocked Jerry's senses. Despite the warmth provided by his suit, he began to imagine the extreme cold had penetrated his suit and started to shiver. A sudden feeling of isolation and emptiness and a distinct feeling that he didn't belong here overwhelmed him. He could see nothing of the surface beyond his feet, already covered by a cloud of dust. He closed his eyes to gather his senses and, opening them, searched his surroundings. All that he could make out was the distant Walnut Mountains weakly brightened by the sun. As his eyes adjusted to the dim light, he searched the heavens for something familiar. The Milky Way extended from horizon to horizon and glowed brightly against the pitch-black but star-studded firmament. The brightest single object other than the sun was a brilliant bluish star situated a few degrees above the rim of Gamma Crater. Jerry assumed that it must be Neptune and a smaller yellowish star just above it would be Uranus. Jupiter and Saturn glowed several degrees higher. He searched in vain for the blue star that would be Earth, but couldn't find it. After a few minutes, Jerry's eyes had adjusted to the dark and he could finally distinguish surface features from the sky. The Milky Way shone bright enough to cast its own weak shadow across the gray powdery ground. Dr. Vincent suggested that they should turn on their helmet lights and begin to shuffle away from Sally. Jerry's headlamp only penetrated a few yards, and except for a few fist-size rocks, there was nothing to grab his attention. Despite the low gravity and level surface, walking on Sedna proved to be a challenge. Trudging along a surface covered with a deep grainy powder reminded Jerry of walking without snowshoes in deep snow back in the Sierra Nevada Mountains. Each time he took a step forward, his boots kicked up a cloud of dust that fell back to the ground in slow motion. Jerry filled a sample container with the gray dust and placed two fist-size rocks in his backpack as Dr. Vincent took several samples of the thin atmosphere at various heights above ground.

They walked about ½ mile, but finding nothing of interest they decided to return to Sally. When they returned, Saul inserted their soil samples into the mass spectrometer and nuclear magnetic resonance machines. The analysis showed Jerry's soil samples consisted mostly of silicates and frozen nitrogen, methane, and water ice. The two rocks were igneous pyroxene (calcium magnesium iron aluminum silicate). The atmospheric samples were mostly nitrogen and methane gas, with a trace of oxygen and carbon dioxide.

"Exactly as expected, and not different from the material in the Gamma Crater," Saul commented.

Peter tried to raise the SIO, but the only response was static.

"I guess the repeater hasn't turned on yet, and since we are below the rim of the Gamma Crater with no orbiting satellites to relay our signal, we will be out of contact until we can place a repeater transmitter on top of the Walnut Ridge," Saul explained.

"Can't we contact Tesla which is in orbit around Sedna?" John asked.

"Unfortunately for us, Tesla is in a low synchronous orbit west of the SIO where it can keep constant contact with Earth, and isn't visible from this location," Peter explained.

Sally continued across the surface and arrived at the base of the Walnut Mountains as the sun set. The imposing Walnut Range cliffs rose abruptly from the ground, affording no chance for Sally to climb over to the other hemisphere. Peter drove north along the base looking for a pass, and after searching for 20 km, a dip in the ridge suggested a potential passage.

"This is a good spot to rest for a few hours and resume our climb up the mountain at sunrise," Peter suggested.

Five hours later, Sally began the steep climb up the pass leading to the Walnut Mountains' ridgeline. Despite the reduced gravity on Sedna and Sally's powerful electric motors, she struggled to gain altitude. When they finally made it to the top, a second range parallel to the first and separated by a 15-km wide valley floor greeted them. The shadow created by the Walnut Range did not allow the morning sun to penetrate the valley below, yet sunlight allowed them to scan the eastern mountain range. Peter searched for a pass, but none was visible. Bill deployed the second relay transmitter, which came on line but because the other transmitter remained off, communication with the SIO was still not possible. They began the climb down to the valley floor, but because the valley side was even steeper than the climb from the Metros Plain, they crept down the mountainside so not to stress Sally's traction past design limits. Glow from the Milky Way provided enough light to see a valley floor different from the surface of the Metros Plain. Despite the weak light, the valley floor appeared peppered with boulder-size rocks. Once on the valley floor, Peter took temperature, gravitational, and magnetic field readings.

"This is strange," he commented. "The temperature outside is 194 degrees centigrade below zero, substantially warmer than our readings on the Metros Plain. The gravity here measures .42 g, and the magnetic field readings are 0.63 gauss. These readings are higher than those we took on the other side of the Walnut Mountain."

As the sun rose overhead and penetrated the valley floor, Peter headed Sally south to search for a pass over the eastern range, but after traveling 50 km they couldn't find one.

"Since we are all tired, and the sun will soon set over the ridge, I suggest we rest here for a few hours and continue our search after the sun rises five hours from now," Dr. Vincent suggested.

Sally came equipped with a small lounge, a kitchen, toilet, and bunks to house ten people. While Ramon prepared the evening meal, Dr. Vincent, Saul Amos, Wendy, and Bill Summerset suited up and ventured outside armed with powerful searchlights. The valley floor was flat and smooth, covered by a few centimeters of powdery soil and, other than the track marks left by Sally, featureless. In the glare of their searchlights, the soil took on a rusty-red color, but in the ambient light it appeared gray and colorless. Evidenced by the dust they raised while walking, the atmosphere in this valley was thicker and deeper than that they experienced on the Metros Plain. Bill grabbed a fistful of the soil and threw it into the sky. It slowly floated back to the ground, suggesting the atmosphere in this valley was several meters thick. Saul took samples of the soil and Dr. Vincent captured samples of the atmosphere. They returned to Sally and Bill analyzed the samples with the mass spectrometer and nuclear magnetic resonance (NMR) equipment.

Bill reported the results. "The valley atmosphere is mostly methane and nitrogen, with a trace of carbon dioxide and eight point four percent of oxygen. We found only a trace of oxygen on the Metros Plain, so this much oxygen in the valley is hard to explain. The soil sample results are also unexpected, very different from that on the Metros Plain. Here we have mostly silicon dioxide, frozen methane, frozen nitrogen, and water ice, with a few iron oxides. The rock samples are a surprise. They are not pyroxene as on the Metros Plain, nor do they contain enough iron oxides to explain the soil's reddish color. There is only a trace of iron oxide in either the rocks or soil, and there is a plethora of heavier metals such as iridium, silver, platinum, lead, and uranium absent in Gamma Crater. The two hemispheres are as different from each other as our moon is from Mars."

"And what could explain the large amount of oxygen in this valley atmosphere?" Peter asked.

"That is another mystery," Bill said. "Yet I have a partial answer for the red color of this hemisphere."

"The most abundant element in our sample and probable source of the red color is tholins (methane-based organic materials). There is also evidence of many other organic compounds. The problem is that the chemical reactions necessary to form tholins require exposure to strong radiation, and the other organic compounds can only form in the presence of liquid water, neither of which now exists on Sedna, at least not for the past billion years. Sedna in some distant past must have been close to our sun, and in fact close enough to melt ice and irradiate methane-based organics."

Wendy looked surprised. "Sedna could never have orbited in our sun's inner solar system and then migrated to its present eccentric orbit that extends outside of the solar system's orbital plane."

"So what then?" Bill asked.

Wendy pondered the question for a minute, and then answered, "We will have to run computer simulations to calculate the dynamics, but my first thought is that Sedna once orbited close to Nemesis, in fact close enough to allow for liquid water to form. Millions or billions of years ago on a close visit to our solar system, our sun stole Sedna from Nemesis."

"That is quite a supposition," Josh quipped.

Wendy replied, "Yes, but since Nemesis was discovered, its orbit around the sun has been worked out. Its eccentric orbit takes it through the Oort Cloud every 26 million years, but once in hundreds of thousands of years it comes quite close to the sun, in fact closer than Sedna's perihelion. It is entirely possible that our sun captured Sedna on one such visit. I will run some computer simulations to see if such a capture is possible."

"If Sedna once orbited close to Nemesis, it could explain the presence of water, tholins, and organic compounds," Bill admitted.

Saul was skeptical. "I find it very hard to believe that Sedna could have been captured by our sun."

"Well, let's wait to see what Wendy's computer simulations have to say about Sedna's past," Dr. Vincent suggested. "In the meantime, we should pack up and find a way through the eastern Walnut ridge to the other side."

The following morning Sally traveled south along the Walnut Valley searching for a pass over the eastern Walnut Mountain range, yet after four hours and another 150km later they could not find a way over the mountain. Peter stopped Sally and used binoculars to search for a pass.

"There is something unusual at the base of that mountain cliff!" Peter exclaimed. "It looks like a cave entrance."

Jerry borrowed the binoculars and searched the cliff, confirming Peter's observation. "It is a cave all right. Peter, let's drive over to it."

"It doesn't look natural," Jerry commented, still looking through the binoculars. "The edges of the entrance are smooth and it appears to have been drilled by some sort of machinery, perhaps a laser or similar device. It looks more like a tunnel than a cave."

"Nevertheless, I have the same impression as Jerry," John Edmund commented as he took his turn with the binoculars. "The cave doesn't look natural, but it could possibly be a lava tube."

Connie Jenkins let out a big sigh, "Ridiculous—a man-made tunnel? We are the first and only humans to explore this valley. We have not seen any lava tubes or evidence of geologically formed caverns. Who could have drilled a tunnel?"

As Sally crept up to the tunnel entrance and drove inside, it became apparent that this was not a naturally formed cave. Wide and high enough to accommodate the rover, the walls of the cave were smooth and looked more like a constructed tunnel than a lava tube. An ubiquitous hazy midst filled the tunnel and prevented Sally's headlights from penetrating more than 10 yards ahead. As they drove 35 yards inside the tunnel, John took a reading of the atmosphere. The pressure was nearly one atmosphere, and the oxygen content was 16 percent. The temperature was a mild 72 degrees Fahrenheit.

"The conditions inside this tunnel are impossible to explain," Bill said. "The atmospheric composition is similar to that back on Earth. The temperature is comfortable, the pressure is nearly one atmosphere, and the oxygen level is high enough for us to breathe without spacesuits. I cannot explain what warms and keeps this atmosphere confined inside the tunnel. The good news is that we can go outside Sally without donning our helmets and rebreathers."

Peter drove Sally another 300 meters inside to where the tunnel suddenly made a left turn and then in another twenty meters came to an abrupt end. Everyone gasped, unable to comprehend what emerged through the midst at the end of the tunnel.

"Oh, my God, what is that?" Peter exclaimed breathlessly.

Not quite believing what their eyes told them, the team gathered around the front window and stared unbelieving at the object only four meters ahead. Dominating the end of the tunnel was a highly polished metal panel, about 2 meters wide and 4 meters high. A 30 cm-wide dull gray frame bordered the panel on the top and on each side, while the bottom of the panel rested on the floor of the tunnel. Stunned and at a loss for words, the team silently stared at the panel.

"It looks like a door," Wendy finally said.

"I don't think it's a door," Saul Amos opined. "How could it be a door here on Sedna, and there are no apparent hinges that would attach a door to the frame. It could just be a panel or wall intended to close off the end of the tunnel."

"Panel, wall, or door … it is not natural," Wendy said.

It seemed unwise to leave their helmets behind, but Bill convinced them it would be safe to do so. Jerry and Judy Stein climbed outside clad in coveralls, jackets, boots, and gloves. In the bright glare of Sally's headlights, the first observation Judy made was that the soil on the tunnel floor looked very different from that on the valley floor. It had the consistency and color of beach sand. Judy took samples of the soil and gave them to Isake. Upon analysis, the sandy soil was pure silicon dioxide.

Peter turned on Sally's high-intensity floodlights, which then bathed the tunnel in bright light. Jerry ran his gloved hand over the object and searched for hinges or something that might indicate if it was a door or just a panel. If it was a door, it was featureless with no signs of hinges, a handle, or other means of entry.

After a few minutes Peter asked, "So, Jerry, what is it?"

"What it is doesn't really matter," Jerry commented to those back in Sally. "The point is that door or panel, humans didn't place it here."

After another minute of silence, Dr. Vincent chose his words carefully.

"This discovery changes everything we thought we knew about Sedna or for that matter about our place in the universe. Personally, I am having a very difficult time imagining the impact that this discovery will have on the UWSF folks, and for that matter everyone back on Earth. Some intelligent and advanced beings, certainly not humans, drilled this tunnel and placed this panel or door at the end of the tunnel. For the past two hundred and fifty years, we have been searching without success for signs of intelligent life in our galaxy. Many feel that we are alone in this part of the Milky Way, and now we are faced with irrefutable proof that we are indeed not alone. This is the greatest discovery in the past millennia."

Jerry agreed. "Humans first landed on Sedna only a decade ago and we are the first to have explored this part of Sedna. Our species certainly could not have made this tunnel and placed this panel here."

"If this is a door, then we have to figure out how to open it," Bill said.

"And if so, what could be behind it?" Wendy added.

"Let's go outside and have a closer look," Josh suggested.

Jerry, Saul Amos, and Bill went outside dressed only in work suits, boots, and gloves. The panel was so highly polished that their reflections mirrored from it. Jerry removed his gloves and gingerly moved his bare hand slowly over the surface of the panel, scanning from side to side and top to bottom.

"It seems slightly warm to the touch and is amazingly smooth and highly polished," he reported. He scanned the door with the ultrasonic probe, but it only indicated solid metal. Then he turned on his X-Ray probe and swept it over the entire surface. "The door is solid, one piece of an unknown metal 23 cm thick. There are no detectable seams or voids. I can find no signs of hinges, a key pad, lock, or other means of entry. There is only a 0.2 cm space between the door and the frame, although the bottom is separated from the floor by 0.5 cm."

Jerry stepped aside to allow Bill to examine the door with his portable Nuclear Magnetic Resonance probe and portable magnetic resonance spectrometer. Bill selected a spot in the center of the door, took a reading, then selected a spot over the frame and took a second reading. "The door is composed of an amalgam of stainless steel, titanium, and cobalt. I will send the data to Isake inside Sally for further analysis. The frame is composed of copper and palladium. We should obtain a small sample of each to place in Sally's mass spectrometer to confirm these readings."

Saul turned on his high-speed diamond drill and attempted to make a small hole in the door to obtain a sample, but the drill couldn't even scratch the door, let alone penetrate it. He then attempted to obtain a sample from the doorframe with the same result.

"Whatever metallurgical process by which this door and frame were manufactured is beyond our present drills to penetrate. I cannot even scratch it," he admitted.

"Let's try the plasma torch," Bill suggested.

Bill retrieved the plasma torch from Sally and attempted to cut around the door's perimeter, but his torch couldn't even make a burn mark on the door.

"It is going to take much more than a plasma torch to cut into this material," Bill admitted. "The door seems to immediately dissipate any heat generated by my torch. Do we have anything else with us that might help us get inside?"

"Not with us," Jerry responded. "If a plasma torch won't do the job, nothing else we have with us on Sedna or Tesla can do so."

"Do you still insist it is a door?" Saul asked. "I think it is just a panel."

"Yes, I still think it is a door," Jerry responded. "The size, shape, and frame suggest such."

While Bill and Jerry were trying to penetrate the door, Isake Mitera fed the results of Bill's NMR and X-ray data into the computer. The crystalline structure of the cobalt steel and titanium molecular matrix indicated a crystalline alignment and interlocking structure unknown to Earth based metallurgical science.

"This material is unique, and I doubt that we have the machines back at the SIO or Tesla to penetrate this door," Isake advised Dr. Vincent.

"Jerry, can you suggest any other way that we could gain entry to whatever is behind the door with the tools we have with us?" Dr. Vincent asked.

"Not that I know about. Our best bet is to discover an entry portal. Every door has to have a way to open it," Jerry argued.

After a careful search of the door and frame, they couldn't find any sign of a keyhole or entry port. The door was planar and smooth with no indentations.

"Dr. Vincent, the door shows no sign of an entry port or a keyhole," Isake said.

"Then let's have everyone come back inside and have a team meeting," Dr. Vincent suggested.

Josh gathered the team around him in Sally's lounge.

"The goal of this mission is to determine the geology of Sedna; since we are at a loss to penetrate this door or even find a keyhole, there is nothing more we can do here for now. We should return to our original mission."

Judy was perplexed. "But this discovery is much more important than any geological exploration. We should stay and find a way inside."

"It appears that we do not have the technology to penetrate or open this door, so we should return to our original mission and finish our geological studies," Dr. Vincent insisted. "The IAU folks will send a better-equipped expedition to open this door."

"That would take years and we are here … now," Judy argued. "Let's continue trying."

"No, we have done all possible to gain entry through the door. We will return to SIO and perhaps come back on another expedition," Josh concluded. "I need to first talk with the UWSF managers and see what they have to suggest."

The narrow tunnel did not allow Sally to turn around, so Peter backed out until they were again outside. Dr. Vincent again attempted to raise the SIO, but apparently the Gamma repeater transmitter was still not working. They resumed their search for a pass over the eastern Walnut ridgeline, yet after searching for several additional hours, they could not find a way to get over that steep and rugged mountain.

"If the UWSF folks want us to explore the other hemisphere of Sedna, we will have to do so on another expedition and approach that side from the west. It appears the eastern Walnut ridge is impassable from the valley," Dr. Vincent admitted. "Tomorrow we will deploy our seismic equipment to see if there is ice and water beneath the surface, and then after drilling a hole for a small explosive device and obtaining our seismic data, we will return home."

After a twelve-hour trek and another sunrise and sunset, hours later they arrived near the western ridgeline where they first entered the Walnut Valley. Peter noticed an unusual irregular ringed depression in the center of the otherwise flat valley floor. It looked as if in the past it might have been a lake. He decided this would be a good location to deploy the seismometer. Bill and Jerry went outside and, with a small auger, dug a three-meter deep hole where they placed the remote seismometer. Then they walked a hundred meters away and began to dig a second deeper hole for the small explosive. As the auger brought material to the surface, Jerry shoveled the resulting rock and soil away from the hole and deposited it in a pile. In one shovel full of material, he noticed a small translucent blue rock different from all the other rocks he had placed on the pile. About the size and shape of a small potato and partly covered by loose red soil, he picked the rock up and rotated it in his gloved hand for a better look. A small amber-colored bent rod about two centimeters long projected from one end of the rock. Jerry brushed the crumbly red soil away from the rock.

"Bill, come over here and see what I found."

Jerry handed the rock to Bill, who repeatedly turned it over to examine it. "The rock is some sort of crystalline silicate, but what is really interesting is the rod that is imbedded in it."

"What in the hell do you think it is?" Jerry asked.

"The rod looks like fossilized bone," Bill surmised.

Jerry frowned. "How can it be a bone? Are you telling me that this once belonged to a living being?"

"I'm not telling you anything. To me it looks like fossilized bone. Let's take it inside and show it to Saul who is an amateur paleontologist. He will know if it is a bone or just a strange rock."

Once back inside the rover, Bill handed the rock to Saul, who carefully extracted a 4-inch rod from the rock and placed it under a microscope.

"This is definitely a fossilized bone. Where in the world did you find it?"

Jerry frowned. "I found it among the material the auger was bringing to the surface, about 2 meters deep."

By this time, the entire team had gathered around Saul, who then handed the bone to Dr. Vincent.

Josh examined it and then passed it around to the rest of the team.

"Bill, you say you found this in the material extracted from the test hole?"

"Actually, Jerry found it. He was shoveling material away from the test hole when he noticed it imbedded in a translucent blue rock."

Dr. Vincent turned to Saul. "Can you identify the bone?"

"I cannot. Perhaps someone back at the SIO or on Tesla will be able to identify it."

Saul placed the rod in a glass vial and gave it back to Jerry for safekeeping.

Bill reported that his tests of the rock extracted from the test hole indicated that it was composed of silicates and tholins. These compounds require the presence of water when formed. The depression where they found the fossil, if it is a fossil, was once a shallow lake.

"Let's complete our seismic experiment and go home," Dr. Vincent suggested.

"Since we have been unable to cross over the eastern Walnut Ridge, we will have to abandon the plan to circumnavigate Sedna and return the way we came, across the Metros Plain.

They detonated the explosive in the test hole and the seismometer imager sent back a series of 3D images that showed that only 3.2 km below the surface lay a 350-meter thick layer of water ice, and beneath that a 1500-meter deep lake of liquid water. Deeper seismometer data indicated Sedna contained a semiliquid nickel-iron core several hundred kilometers in diameter heated by radioactivity.

Having obtained the geological data, Peter drove to the top of the Walnut range pass and again attempted to raise the SIO. This time they were able to contact the SIO through the Gamma ridge repeater. Dr. Vincent relayed pictures of the door and transmitted all the seismic data that they collected. He said nothing at this time about the supposed fossil. Peter then drove Sally down onto the Metros Plain and the expedition was back at the SIO 15 hours later and two days short of the original mission.

Chapter Five
The Second Expedition

A crowd was waiting in the hangar to greet them as they arrived back at the SIO. The data and pictures they transmitted earlier caused wild excitement with the SIO scientists. As Dr. Vincent climbed down from Sally, Dr. Pinot, the SIO director, greeted him.

"The pictures and data you sent back from the Walnut Ridge are mind-boggling, and have caused a controversy both here and back on Earth. A metal door or panel blocked the end of an artificial tunnel in Walnut Valley? If this is true, it will revise everything we thought we knew about the solar system and our place in the universe. It is the first hard evidence we have ever obtained that we are not alone in this universe and that extraterrestrials have visited our solar system. The message I sent to the UWSF about this discovery contained no details yet caused a sensation back on Earth, and of course they immediately wanted you to debrief them. Meantime, I have scheduled a debriefing meeting in the auditorium for this evening, but I want to debrief the team privately myself before Dr. Vincent sends the details of your discovery to the UWSF folks back on Earth."

"What lies behind that door is more important than the door itself," Dr. Vincent said. "We did everything possible with the tools we had with us to find a way behind that door, but despite our drills and the plasma torch, we were unable to penetrate or find any keyhole or panel. We need to mount a second expedition to the valley to continue our effort to open the door."

Dr. Pinot thought for a moment before answering. "Every door has a key. If none of our tools can open the door, then we simply must find the key. With UWSF permission, I want to authorize a second mission for you and your team to revisit Walnut Valley, but it is up to the UWSF folks.

"I have something else to show you," Dr. Vincent said, and handed the vial containing the fossil to Dr. Pinot.

"What is this?"

"I think it may be a fossilized bone that we found while digging a test hole for the seismometer experiment in Walnut Valley."

"You found this in the ground?"

"We did—about two meters deep, in what we think was an ancient lake bed. I assume you have someone here who is an expert in identifying fossils?"

"Unfortunately we do not have a paleontologist on our staff. Perhaps one of our amateur fossil collectors can identify the item for you. If this is a fossilized bone, it will cause almost as much of a sensation back on Earth as finding the tunnel and door has done."

When the debriefing began, Dr. Vincent recounted details of the entire exploratory mission. Everyone only wanted to hear about the tunnel and the door, so Dr. Vincent began with that discovery, showed photographs, and then spent 15 minutes answering questions about it. Folks were disappointed the team couldn't penetrate or figure out how to open the door, so Josh asked Isake Mitera to explain about the door's unique crystalline structure, yet Isake's explanation didn't convince everyone that this was technology beyond our science and not some man-made object.

Dr. Vincent then asked Wendy to explain her theory about the origins of Sedna. After Wendy offered her theory that Sedna may have once orbited Nemesis, she asked Dr. Edith Carlson, the manager of the Sedna Astronomy Observatory, to catch everyone up-to-date on the latest Nemesis findings. Dr. Carlson, a well-respected and experienced astronomer who had just celebrated her sixtieth birthday, accepted the microphone from Wendy with a warm smile and began her talk.

"I agree with Dr. Wilson's theories about the origin of Sedna. Since its discovery last year, the SIO team has been carefully observing Nemesis and has learned much about this red dwarf companion to our sun. Four point seven billion years ago, Nemesis and our sun formed from the same primordial cloud of hydrogen, helium, and dust. Most suns have companion stars and our sun is no exception to the rule. For years, astronomers suspected that our sun had a companion star but were unable to detect it until the SIO began observations from Sedna and discovered Nemesis. Until the SIO thirty-meter telescope achieved first light, the companion to our sun remained invisible. It is a distant, rather small, cool red dwarf, with about 15 percent of our sun's mass and emits

100,000 times less luminosity. Nemesis orbits our sun in an elongated elliptical path that takes it from its present location more than 2,350 AU from the sun to a perihelion that brings it as close as 25 astronomical units. Every 26 million years Nemesis reaches perigee and as it passes through the Oort Cloud on its way toward the solar system, it sends thousands of comets racing into the inner solar system, some of which collide with Earth. These close encounters vary from 25 AU to 125 AU, and on one particularity close encounter with our solar system 3.8 billion years ago, Nemesis came near enough to disrupt our solar system, causing the orbits of the planets Uranus and Neptune, which initially formed much closer to the sun than their present locations, to switch place and migrate outward. Theia, a small planet the size of Mars that formed in the inner solar system, migrated inward and collided with Earth, a glancing blow that almost destroyed our planet. The resulting debris coalesced to form our moon."

Dr. Carlson paused to show a slide depicting the possible orbits of Nemesis.

"Nemesis probably initially formed with several planets of its own, yet we have detected only one rocky planet that still orbits that sun. Our simulations indicate that after several close encounters, either Nemesis' solar system planetary orbits became so erratic that its member planets were flung out of the Nemesis system into deep space or our sun or planets captured them. Triton, 2012VIP$_{113}$, and Sedna may have originally orbited Nemesis. Leto, Pluto, Charon, and Triton may be examples of other planets ripped from Nemesis or perhaps from other visiting star systems. This theory explains the unusual orbits of these rogue dwarf planets and coincides with Wendy's hypothesis that Sedna is an alien visitor to our solar system. If Sedna was born close to Nemesis, it would explain why it once had a thick warm atmosphere and surface water, and environment where tholins and silicates could form. Yet this explains nothing about the advanced civilization who constructed the tunnel and the impenetrable door on Sedna. Nor can it explain the purpose these visitors had in mind when they constructed the door. Because we have yet to discover other evidence of an advanced civilization on Sedna, my guess is that those who erected the door were not inhabitants but transient alien visitors. We can only answer these questions by opening the door. It is imperative that we mount a second expedition to Walnut Valley as soon as possible."

Applause filled the auditorium and when the audience quieted down, Dr. Pinot took the microphone.

"The door is not the only astounding discovery our geologists made while in Walnut Valley. They found what they believe is a fossil bone beneath the surface."

Then Dr. Pinot took out the vial that contained the alleged fossil and placed it under a camera, which displayed it on the overhead video screen.

"The discovery of an actual fossil on Sedna is almost as difficult to accept as is the tunnel and door. We have not yet analyzed it, yet under a microscope it certainly appears to be a focalized bone. If there is anyone at the SIO versed in paleontology who can help identify the fossil, please tell Dr. Vincent. Dr. Vincent will immediately notify UWSF about this discovery and ask for permission to conduct another expedition to the Walnut Valley to search for more fossils."

Dr. Pinot then ended the meeting.

After Dr. Vincent's debriefing telecom, the UWSF managers and the folks back on Earth were in a buzz about the door and the possibility of a fossil discovered on Sedna. Newspapers on Earth ran headlines that read "We Are Not Alone." Some scientists and government leaders remained skeptical, although the pictures and data the geologic team sent back left little room for debate. The tunnel and door were not natural nor made by man. The idea of a fossil on Sedna drew immediate criticism from paleontologists who argued that any conclusions should wait until they analyze the Sedna "fossil bone" back here on Earth.

For 200 years, various investigations like SETI (the Search for Extraterrestrial Intelligence) searched for intelligent radio transmissions, evidence of extraterrestrial aliens. Finding nothing, SETI shut the project down and the team concluded that aliens did not live close enough to Earth for their broadcasts to reach us yet, or that they had not invented the technology necessary to broadcast powerful radio or laser signals.

The former SETI managers lobbied the United World leaders to authorize another expedition to the Walnut Valley and the tunnel. The secrets that remain hidden behind that door would be the greatest discovery of the modern age. The United World leaders authorized the UWSF to send the Sedna geological team on a second expedition, and the managers sent instructions to Dr. Pinot that Dr. Vincent should immediately organize a second expedition to Walnut Valley.

Josh decided that he needed to recruit some new members for the second expedition and this mission should make use of both rovers. Technicians reequipped Sally and prepared a second rover named Sam for the journey to Walnut Valley. Dr. Vincent expanded his team to thirteen members, selecting physician Dr. Connie Jenkins, Judy Stein, Saul Amos, Wendy Wilson, John Edmunds, Peter Ramos, and Isake Mitera from the first expedition. He asked Jerry to drive Sam, and Peter to drive Sally. The new team members recruited from SIO observatory employees included linguistic and cryptanalysis expert Dana Ingstrom, anthropologist Dick Carlson, electrical engineer Jim Dean, and molecular metallurgist Michael Penobscot. Dr. Vincent split the team into Sally and Sam members. Accompanying Jerry in Sam were Judy, Saul, Dana, John, and Michael. Dr. Vincent assigned Isake, Jim, Peter, Wendy, Dick, and Connie to ride with Peter and him in Sally.

Michael brought along more powerful tools lent from the SIO—a plasma torch and an abrasive jet, a high-pressure jet of water and abrasive diamonds designed to cut through hard materials. Either tool could cut through 2-inch hardened steel or titanium plates as if they were butter.

****

July 2120

The second expedition plan was to circumnavigate Sedna by heading west rather than east, cross over the Bandar Quarter, and then drop into the Walnut Valley by surmounting the Walnut Ridge. They hoped to find a pass over that ridge, set up a base camp in Walnut Valley, and then visit the tunnel again. Equipped with enough food, water, and oxygen for a ten-day mission, Sally and Sam drove over the Gamma Crater rim and onto the Bandar Quarter plains west of the SIO. The Bandar plains contained more craters and lava ridges than did the Metros Plain. Nine hours and a second sunrise later, they crossed over a small rise where the landscape abruptly changed. Even in the weak sunlight, the soil looked distinctly red rather than gray. They stopped to take instrument readings and collect soil and rock samples. The measurements and samples were different from those taken on the Metros Plain but similar to those taken in the Walnut Valley. The reddish permafrost soil consisted of tholins and silicates with only a smattering of iron oxides. They drilled another exploratory hole into the frozen ground and at a depth of 60 meters discovered liquid water. After resting for fifteen hours and traveling through another sunset and sunrise, 30 hours after leaving the SIO the ridge of the Walnut Mountains came into view. The mountains stretched from north to south across the entire western horizon of Sedna. Peter used his telescope to search for a pass, but none was immediately visible. After arriving at the base of the Walnut Mountains they traveled northward, continuing to search for a mountain pass—but they didn't find a pass where they could safely cross over. They continued north until, when almost to the north pole, they came to a wide gap that bisected the Walnut Mountains as if they as if it had been cleaved with a giant ax. A 50-meter deep, 100-meter wide ditch began 3 km from the base of the mountain and then continued across the Walnut Valley, plowing through both the eastern and the western Walnut Mountain ranges and out onto the Metros Plain.

"It looks as if an asteroid plowed into Sedna with a glancing blow eons ago and created this ditch," John suggested.

"It is strange the folks on Tesla haven't noticed this ditch before," Peter said.

"Not so strange at all," Dr. Vincent responded. "They parked Tesla in a low synchronous orbit above the SIO so it could keep in contact with Earth. They cannot view either the north or south poles of Sedna from that orbit. They just never saw this gap in the mountains."

Regardless, the gap provided Sally and Sam with easy access into the valley.

As the rovers entered the valley, the hydraulic pump temperature indicator on Sam began to red-line. Jerry shut Sam down and called Peter Ramos.

"Pete, there is a problem with our hydraulic pump. Do you have a spare pump onboard Sally?"

"Unfortunately we do not," Peter reported. "I'll come over and have a good look at your pump and see what the problem could be. There might be a few pump spare parts already onboard Sam."

Removing the pump from the engine compartment proved more difficult than expected. Access to the outside compartment that housed the pump required donning a space suit and gloves, and the gloves hampered Peter's dexterity. After struggling with this task for over two hours, he finally extracted the defective pump and took it inside Sam to see if he could repair it. A crack split the pump impeller, and despite a careful search through the spare parts compartment, he couldn't find a spare impeller.

"It appears that for now Sam is unrepairable," Peter told Dr. Vincent. "We will have to transfer all personnel and equipment over to Sally and leave Sam here. We can rescue it on a future trip."

"This is exactly why we brought along two machines," Dr. Vincent commented. "If we didn't have a second rover, we would be in real trouble."

Although all thirteen members and their equipment were now on board Sally, no one complained about the cramped quarters. The team drove Sally south along the Walnut Valley until eight hour later they arrived at the tunnel entrance.

On entering the tunnel, the atmosphere pressure, oxygen content, and temperature inside measured the same as it had on the previous visit, and those venturing outside didn't need to wear space suits. They parked in front of the door and Judy, John, Michael, Isake, and Jerry went outside Sally to examine it with their analytical equipment. John probed the door carefully from top to bottom with his magnetic, neutrino, and X-ray diffraction scanners. Unfortunately, none of his instruments revealed a port or void in the door, or any hinges in the frame. The ambient temperature in the tunnel was 72 degrees F but the door's temperature remained at 104 degrees F.

"Something inside is warming this door," Michael Penobscot claimed.

After taking some time to analyze the scans, Isake and Michael prepared their cutting torches.

After several attempts to cut into the door or its frame, Michael was frustrated. The plasma torch and abrasive jet had no effect on the door. The object wouldn't allow even the smallest cut or scratch to mar its pristine surface and instantly dissipated the 4,000-degree heat produced by the plasma torch. The abrasive jet couldn't mark the door or frame, even when they used diamond dust as the abrasive.

"This is the most impenetrable material I have ever worked on," Michael said in total frustration. "The metal is homogenous, structured like a single molecule, and harder than a diamond. It absorbs and dissipates nearly 100 percent of incident energy without increasing its own internal temperature. We have no metallurgy on earth that can compare to this."

The infrared spectroscopy (IRS) and nuclear magnetic resonance (NMR) probes revealed a crystalline structure with the individual iron and titanium crystals combined with carbon in a perfectly interlocked crystalline matrix. "The metal acts like one giant crystal. It is a perfect thermodynamic blackbody radiator, unaffected and impervious to our best efforts to heat it or cut into it," John reported.

Jerry nodded. "Our only hope then is to look for a key or some key lock. Every door has a lock. Those who made this door had to have a way to open it."

Judy Stein suggested they examine the door with her ultrasonic probe. Michael was skeptical.

"I don't know what you expect to find with your ultrasonic probe that our IRS and NMR probes didn't reveal, but have a go at it."

As Judy and Jerry prepared the probe to scan the door, Isake, John, and Michael returned to Sally to view their results using the more sophisticated analytical software in the rover computer.

With the ultrasonic probe, Judy set the probe frequency to scan over the door back and forth from 20 kHz to 60 kHz and began moving from left to right starting at the top of the door as she watched the monitor. She methodically moved the probe downward while spending a minute or so with each scan. When she was about halfway to the floor, an orange isosceles triangle, about 25 mm on a side, briefly flashed on and then off from inside the door. Leaving the scanner in place, she set the scanner frequency to step over the entire frequency range, pausing briefly in two hundred and fifty hertz increments. The triangle reappeared at 35.75 kHz and remained on until the frequency increased to 36.25 kHz. She locked the frequency to 36 kHz and increased the power. The triangle was diffuse but visible and glowed with a soft orange florescence. When she moved the scanner away or changed the frequency, the triangle disappeared.

"Jerry, have a look at this!" Judy exclaimed. "It could be a key. Please ask Michael to turn off Sally's front lights."

In the dimmed light, the triangle fluoresced bright enough to be clearly visible.

"Why didn't we see this on the first expedition when I scanned the door with the ultrasonic probe?" Jerry asked.

"Probably because the triangle isn't visible in Sally's bright lights, and the scanner quickly swept past 36 kHz," Judy suggested. "I almost missed it myself on this pass."

Sally sent a picture of the triangle to those inside Sally. Dr. Vincent's voice boomed from the communicator. "You've discovered the keyhole!" he said excitedly. Saul, Peter, and Dana Ingstrom immediately joined Judy and Jerry outside. On closer examination in the dimmed light, Jerry could make out a few symbols inside the triangle.

"Dana, please have a closer look at these symbols," Jerry suggested.

The dozen symbols or characters were reminiscent of ancient cuneiform. They varied in size, with the largest at the apex of the triangle and less than 5 mm high. Dana made a pencil sketch in her notebook of each character, carefully copying their size and relative position inside the triangle. "I'll have to return to my computer to analyze these."

"We have a keyhole with instructions," Jerry said. "Now all we need is a key."

Back inside Sally, everyone gathered around Dana as she worked on her computer interpretation of the symbols.

After a few minutes, the computer had translated the symbols on the first line. "This is weird, but the first line reads something like, "Open Me," Dana reported.

"Just like in *Alice in Wonderland*," Judy commented. "Will the door lead us down the rabbit hole?"

"Well, that is the best translation that my language comparator can come up with," Dana replied. "The rest of the message will need a lot more translation work. Right now it is pure gibberish."

"It may be instructions for opening the door," Jerry suggested.

"Let Dana do her work," Dr. Vincent suggested, and motioned for everyone to return to the lounge. After everyone sat down, Dr. Vincent said, "We have learned something valuable about the door. It responded to an ultrasonic scan. This could be the way these aliens communicate."

"Or it could just be the way they designed their keys," Jerry added.

"It is interesting the door did not respond to any of our RF or X-Ray, or neutrino beam scans, but does so to ultrasonic," Michael commented.

"Any advanced civilization capable of interspace travel and with the sophistication to build this tunnel and door would have also designed a way to open it that is more intricate than just a keyhole and key. Yet using ultrasonic sound to unlock a door is low-tech, yet obviously the way they designed it," Dr. Vincent said.

"Over a hundred and fifty years ago we used such low-tech technology to change channels on a remote TV changer," Jim Dean commented.

"I saw one of those once in a San Francisco museum," Jerry said. "The device struck little rods each tuned to a specific ultrasonic frequency. It was a clever but archaic technology."

Meanwhile, Dana had translated the remaining symbols depicted in the triangle and called everyone over to her computer to witness the screen.

The message wasn't a code or encrypted in some manner, nor did it consist of instructions.

"It is a mathematical formula: $X_n=X_n+X_{n-1}$, and so on," she said. "This is a sequence of Fibonacci numbers, like 1, 1, 2, 3, 5, 8, 13, 21, and 34. I suggest we return to the door, awaken the key lock, and use the scanner to program these numbers into the key lock."

"I will have to modify the Ultrasonic Scanner to modulate the 36 kHz carrier," Jim Dean said.

Jim adjusted the ultrasonic scanner and returned to the door with Dana, Dr. Vincent, Jerry, Wendy, Peter, and Dick Carlson. Jim awakened the key lock triangle with the ultrasonic scanner, and then with his hand computer fed the sequence of Fibonacci numbers into the scanner.

Jim entered each Fibonacci number, pausing before entering the next number in the sequence. When he entered the sixth number in the sequence and before he could enter the next number, the door began to shimmer and fade, growing more and more transparent until it had disappeared. It didn't open or slide into the wall—it just dissolved. The team peered into the room that lay beyond the now-opened portal, but they couldn't see anything. The interior was inky black. Jerry turned on his high-power flashlight and shined it inside. The darkness swallowed the flashlight beam, revealing nothing inside.

They all stood outside the door peering into the empty blackness.

"I guess someone should just step through the portal," Josh finally suggested.

Jerry was the first person to do so, closely followed by Dr. Vincent and then Isake and Peter. As they crossed the portal threshold, a soft indigo glow began to radiate from the surrounding walls and in a few seconds, the light revealed the interior of a large, domed chamber. Jerry judged the chamber to be about 30 meters deep and half again as wide. The dome-shaped ceiling rose to a maximum of 10 meters, and the black mirrorlike walls reflected their images. Jerry's temperature gauge read 72 degrees. The air smelled dank and musty, but not disagreeably so.

Dr. Vincent looked around the room in amazement.

"This chamber is old—very old," he commented. "Nevertheless, it has managed to preserve this comfortable environment for perhaps millions of years. I can only wonder about the source of energy that powers and maintains it."

As the interior continued to brighten, Wendy stepped into the chamber and looked around, "Nothing but an empty room," she said.

"Not entirely empty," Jerry corrected as the rest of the team entered the room.

A six-sided black marble pedestal occupied the center of the room, and next to it sat a four-foot-high empty black marble table. On top of the pedestal rested a dark glass sphere about 40 centimeters in diameter.

The polished pedestal, almost two meters high and 36 centimeters wide on each side, supported the sphere. Dr. Vincent walked over to the pedestal and carefully examined each side for some writing, but there were no marks on the surface. A dozen 2-cm diameter ports randomly placed around the sphere reminded Dr. Vincent of a planetarium projector.

"See if you can activate it," Dana suggested.

Dr. Vincent looked for buttons or some other hint of controls, but nothing of the kind was visible. He passed his hand gently over the surface of the sphere.

"It feels slightly warm," he said. "Please hand me the ultrasonic probe." As he activated the probe programmed to 36 kHz and passed it over the sphere, it began to make a soft humming sound and then sprang into life. A beam of green laser light sprang from one of the ports and moved about the room, momentarily resting on each individual, and then paused on each of the instruments that they carried with them.

"The machine is scanning us and our equipment," Peter said.

After a few seconds, the beam shut off and the room darkened. The dome displayed a firmament of stars and asterisms, yet not one familiar to anyone on the team.

"Just like a planetarium display, only much more detailed," Dr. Vincent said.

"It is not like the sky above Walnut Valley or Earth," Wendy commented. "I don't recognize any of these asterisms. Nevertheless it could be the sky as viewed from the alien's home planet."

"I think the asterism with the bright orange star might be Betelgeuse in Orion the hunter and the star diagonally across from it could be Bellatrix," Saul offered. "You can see the three belt stars and the sword stars, as well and the hip stars Rigel and Saiph, yet the constellation is distorted and different from the one I am familiar with back on Earth. To the left and below Bellatrix is a brilliant blue star that could only be Sirius, but while Sirius is the brightest star in our constellations, this star is even brighter, hence closer to this alien planet."

Wendy agreed with Saul's assessment. Then the chamber, the pedestal, and sky dissolved and they found themselves standing on a dirt road that traced its origin into a brightly-lit valley surrounded by distant orange-tinted mountains. No one from the team spoke. The scene was not like a projection but to all their senses very real. The only sound was the wind as it blew across the valley. The light breeze that caressed their cheeks was hot, arid, and to Jerry the air smelled of parched sand. The soft sand that covered the road yielded to their feet leaving shallow footprints as they walked. The reddish-brown valley floor, barren and lifeless, undulated in a series of low sand dunes and shallow depressions devoid of anything green. Two suns hung in the sky, each casting their separate shadows onto the road. The larger of the two suns, orange with four times the diameter of our own sun, painted the landscape in a harsh orange glow and bathed them in uncomfortable waves of radiant heat that left them wishing for shade. Hanging overhead and adding to the surrealism of the scene was an intensely bright bluish-white second sun much smaller than the orange sun.

"Where the hell are we?" Jim finally asked.

"We're still in the projection chamber," Jerry assured him. "This is a 3D holographic projection, a clever illusion."

"It looks and feels so real that it's hard to believe that it's only a projection," Wendy commented.

Dana called their attention to a city of blue glass skyscrapers bathed by the blue sun in the far distance.

"Just like the emerald city in the Wizard of Oz, except its blue," Dana said.

Some distance down the road, they noticed a figure approaching them. Dressed in a pale blue ankle-length gown, the being stood about four feet tall with ebony skin and an egg-shaped chinless head topped by wavy golden hair. Perched on a skinny neck, the head appeared oversized for the small, frail body. Pink lips outlined a round mouth and two slits below the broad forehead suggested two widely spaced eyes. When the being was only a few feet away, the slits opened and revealed small intensely blue eyes that seemed to stare right through each of them.

The creature extended its long thin arms outward palms up in a universal gesture of peace. It attempted a smile and then the mouth opened, revealing a toothless interior with no tongue. The being began to speak in a melodious voice that came not through the air but within each person's head.

"Welcome to Prestinos," the voice said in perfect English, "or at least this is how Prestinos looked eons ago. Our machine has scanned your instruments and interpreted your language, so now it is possible to speak to you and tell our story in your own tongue."

"Is it a projection or a real person?" Dana asked.

"It's only a projection," Dr. Vincent answered.

The figure continued after placing its hands to its side.

"You have discovered the archive that we, the Dorian people, left behind on this little planet eons ago. You have voyaged to this place so far from your own world, that it proves your advanced technology and highly developed evolution. Your species is young, having only recently started on your long evolutionary journey. Our species, on the other hand, is ancient, having existed for many millions of your years. We have traveled between the stars for longer than humans have existed. As you begin the next step in your evolutionary history, we wish for you to understand that you are not alone in this wide, vast universe. We are one of many species throughout what you call the Milky Way, yet our story and the reason for our visit to your solar system is a sad one."

"Can all of you hear this?" Dr. Vincent asked. Everyone nodded affirmatively. The voice continued. Dana was trying to record the being and his speech on her transcoder, but later discovered the device had recorded nothing.

"These images show our planet as it was at the time we began our voyage to your solar system, a trip that took many of your centuries. Our own sun, having exhausted its supply of hydrogen, entered its red giant phase, growing huge and making life on our planet unbearable. Our planet was dying and our civilization was dying with it. Soon the sun would expand and envelop our poor planet, baking it to a cinder. Our leaders devised a plan to continue our species by sending several spaceships on long journeys to renew our species on emerging worlds. Our leaders chose three hundred persons to travel to a distant solar system, your solar system to be exact, where we could begin anew. They determined the third planet you call Earth had all the necessary conditions for life: liquid water, a comfortable temperature, a diversity of organisms, and a breathable oxygen atmosphere. We trusted that it could become our new home. Space is so vast and your Earth so distant that we knew our journey would take several generations and that none of the original pioneers who left Prestinos would be alive when our people finally arrived in this system. A desperate plan, but the only choice we had to continue our species."

Again, the creature tried a smile before it continued.

"When we finally arrived on Earth, there was only disappointment for us. We thought the planet would be pristine, ideal for our needs. We were wrong. A thousand years before we arrived, a large asteroid smashed into the planet, causing an ecological disaster. A blanket of dust and ash covered the planet and devastated most plant and animal life. Conditions on Earth and in its atmosphere were not favorable for our species, but it was favorable for a small native species. When we examined the DNA of the few small mammalian species that had survived, we determined that given time and because of the ecological changes, evolution would eventually produce a bipedal intelligent species from these small mammals and result in beings such as you. Our prime directive forbids us from interfering in the natural evolutionary process that occasionally produces intelligent species, and our presence on Earth would certainly do so. For our own sake and for yours, we realized that we had to find a more hospitable home elsewhere in the galaxy. There are millions of worlds similar to Earth throughout this galaxy, some early in their own evolutionary process, and others like our own world that are dying and have become hostile to life. Unfortunately, it will require another long journey and many more generations before we arrive at a world suitable to sustain and grow our species. You are relative infants in the cosmological evolution of the universe and have much to learn. We wish you well on your own evolutional journey."

The being paused, and then looked intently at each person.

"As we exited your solar system on our long journey, we created this archive and left you a gift, a marvelous gift that will enhance your technology and allow your species to live longer and become active space explorers no longer confined to this solar system. We knew if you had developed the technology to arrive here at the fringe of your solar system, your technology had advanced so you could appreciate and use our gift. Your sun will not exhaust its supply of hydrogen for several billions of years yet to come, so your species can continue to evolve for many eons."

The Dorian again paused searching for a sign that they understood.

"You will find our gift in a niche in the back wall of this cavern. Protected inside the container is our gift that we freely share with you. Our technology will allow you to advance your civilization in many wonderful ways, including cures for diseases, extending longevity, a better understanding of physics and the cosmos, and a means of power generation and travel that will allow you to join the family of sentient beings who roam throughout this galaxy. It will provide your species with great wonders, but if misused it can also create great harm. Please use our gift wisely."

The Dorian extended one arm and waved with its long spindly fingers as the entire apparition dissolved. They found themselves again standing in front of the pedestal and sphere in the dimly lit cavern.

Without hesitation, Dr. Vincent and Jerry walked to the back wall and found the 3x2 foot niche in the wall. On a shelf inside the niche sat a cube, twenty-three centimeters on each side. Josh shined his flashlight into the niche to get a better look. The object was black, blacker than anthracite coal, with a remarkably smooth and polished surface, yet that surface provided no reflections of the room or the team and absorbed the beam from his flashlight. Jerry couldn't get a clear view of the cube lit only by the soft blue glow emanating from the back of the niche, so he reached inside the niche, carefully placed his hands around the cube, and bought it out into the room. The object seemed surprisingly light for its size so he assumed it must be hollow. It also felt warm in his hands.

"It is not heavy," Jerry commented as he rotated the cube, examining all six sides. "It is smooth and perfectly square."

"Place the cube on the marble table," Josh suggested.

They carefully measured the width of each side and the length of each diagonal. Limited only by their instrument's resolution, all six sides measured the same. There were no markings or an obvious way to get inside the cube, which appeared made from the same metallic material as the door. With no visible marks, dents, icons or writing, and no obvious way to open it, Jerry asked if anyone had an idea that might allow them to do so.

Isake offered an idea.

"Jim, please bring the ultrasonic device over here and pass it over each side of the cube as we did to open the door."

Jim scanned each side of the cube as they had done with the door but no red triangle or other markings appeared.

"Hold the ultrasonic probe over each side of the cube and send the Fibonacci sequence."

Jim did so but the cube still did not respond.

"Let's take it inside the rover where there is better light," Josh suggested.

As soon as the last person left the Dorian chamber, the door that up to this point had remained open now shimmered back into a solid object, and the door once again sealed the entrance to the chamber.

Dr. Vincent thoroughly examined the cube in the bright lights inside the rover, and then he let everyone have a turn to hold it.

"So, this is their gift to us?" Wendy mocked as she turned the object over. "Without explicit instructions, how are we supposed to unwrap this so-called gift?"

Bill and Jerry took the black cube to the back of the rover and scanned it with the x-ray diffraction, mass-spectrometer, and crystal analyzers.

Bill examined the X-ray photographs. "There is a seven-centimeter diameter sphere in the center of the cube composed of titanium and vanadium, a substance different from which the cube is made. I cannot even begin to make out the metallurgy of the cube, and this molecular crystallogy is something that I have never before seen."

Peter tried to warm the cube with an infrared heater, but the surface temperature remained at 104 degrees Fahrenheit.

After a few minutes, he offered an opinion. "The cube is not radioactive, so that can't be the source of the internal heating. It absorbs and emits almost all forms of incident radiation, including infrared, visible light, ultraviolet, and microwaves. It is close to qualifying as a "so-called" perfect black body radiator, which means that it fully absorbs almost all incident radiation and emits nearly all that it receives, enabling the object to regulate its temperature at 104 degrees. I noted the temperature in the niche was a comfortable 72 degrees, yet the cube remained above that ambient temperature."

"This metal is way beyond my ability to understand it," Bill admitted. "We don't have the proper equipment here on the rover to analyze the cube. The lab back on Tesla has access to better equipment. I suggest we take the cube back to the SIO and then to Tesla for testing."

"The big mystery is that if the Dorians wanted to leave us a gift, then why have they made it so difficult for us to get inside the cube?" Jim asked.

"That is an excellent question," Dr. Vincent said. "Jerry … are you sure there was not some writing inside the niche?"

"After extracting the cube, I carefully searched the niche, but there was nothing to suggest writing or graphics."

"That is curious. You'd think the Dorians would have left some instructions for accessing the cube," Josh said. "Nevertheless, we should finish our mission."

"We will have time in the next few months on Sedna to participate in other missions and further explore this hemisphere. We will return to the valley and chamber on our next mission," Jerry said

"And it will take almost three years of travel before we arrive back home, plenty of time to try to understand the Dorian cube and find some way to access the sphere inside and extract our gift," Peter added.

"Or perhaps we will have to wait until we return to Earth where we will have access to the fully equipped labs at the USAW outside Las Vegas," Isake added. "They can nondestructively open anything."

The return journey over the Walnut Mountains and across the Metros plane on Sally was uneventful. Peter was able to contact the SIO from the repeater installed on the Walnut summit, and told them about discovering the tunnel and door and that they were unable to open the door. Peter sent all the data they had gathered and pictures of the tunnel and door and attempted to send the recording of the Dorian encounter, but none of their recorders had been able to capture the Dorian holographic message. All that Peter could do was to describe the Dorian and his message.

Dozens of SIO folks crowded into the hangar to greet the geology team when they arrived. They bombarded Dr. Vincent with questions, mostly about the Dorian cube, which they begged to examine. Josh said he would present the cube in a meeting. He then turned to Jerry and asked him to take personal charge of the Dorian cube.

"For the rest of our time here on Sedna and our journey back home, I want you alone to assume responsibility for the cube. Keep it in your personal care at all times." Jerry accepted his duty and the next day placed the cube inside a stainless steel, airtight insulated transport box slightly larger than the cube.

Responding to the crowd, Josh promised to hold a meeting in the auditorium that evening where he would display the cube. Because the SIO was an observatory and as such did not have a metallurgical lab, the equipment they did have on hand was unable to analyze or open the cube. Over the next few days, Jerry, Isake, and Bill used the shuttle to travel to Tesla where they had access to the ship's metallurgical laboratory. Unfortunately, the lab did not yield any extra information about the impermeable cube nor could the Tesla scientists suggest a way to open it.

Within an hour after their arrival back at the SIO, Dr. Vincent sent a detailed message to the UWSF headquarters back on Earth describing the tunnel and the chamber behind the door with a holographic projector, and the cube. He related the text of Dorian holographic message, the promise of a wonderful gift the Dorians left behind inside of a protective cube that to this point had resisted every attempt to open it. The response on Earth to their Dorian discovery was momentous. Translated into every language, the news read, "We Are Not Alone." Debate flourished about the Sedna information that the UWSF released to the press. Several scientists suggested methods to open the cube and pontificated about the promised gift. Every one of their suggestions to open the cube had either already been tried or failed to make any headway. The UWSF director wanted Tesla and the geological team to return home with the cube as soon as possible, yet he realized that their mission was to remain on Sedna for a few more months and recommended three more geological expeditions for Josh's team during their remaining time on Sedna.

Chapter Six
Homeward Bound

Dr. Vincent and his geological team remained on Sedna for another five months and made three additional explorations of the Sedna surface, including a rescue of the Sam rover and a second visit to the Dorian chamber. Although the door again admitted them into the chamber, this time the projector did not respond to their attempts to activate it, so they learned nothing new about the Dorian chamber or a way to access the cube on this visit.

Their efforts to find more fossils on the Metros Plain, the Walnut Valley, and Bandar Quarter were unsuccessful. Each excavation produced nothing. Disappointed, they returned to the lakebed where they first discovered the fossil, and after digging several holes, they did find several other small fossils and broken pieces of fossils. Dick Carlson, who did not believe in coincidences, questioned how they could have discovered the original fossil with a single exploratory test hole. Saul suggested the center of the funnel-shaped lakebed provided the most likely place for bones to collect, and that was where they had dug their original test hole. The dozen newly discovered fossilized bones were from small animals and not from the same species as the first fossil. Dick carefully wrapped all his samples for the three-year transport home where paleontologists back on Earth could study them in detail.

Over the next three months, the geological team conducted two more geological trips across Sedna, collected samples, conducted additional seismic tests, and spent their remaining time analyzing their data and journaling their explorations on Sedna. Finally it was time to prepare for the almost three-year transit back to Earth, and the Tesla crew began refueling, outfitting, and preparing for the long journey home. A week before Tesla's scheduled departure from Sedna orbit, Dr. Vincent and his team said good-bye to the SIO folks and boarded their shuttle for the short trip back to the starship where Captain Ferguson and his crew warmly greeted them. Except for a few visits to the SIO, most of the Tesla crew had remained on board for the entire twelve months the geologists were on Sedna.

******

February 2121

Three years and four months after leaving the moon's orbit, Starship Tesla fired the VLSMIR engine and gently eased away from Sedna. Alone in the observation room, Jerry felt the gentle tug of acceleration and watched as the velocity meter slowly increased and Sedna began to recede in the window. Jerry was elated when Wendy finally joined him one hour later. In the twelve months that the geological team had been on Sedna, Wendy and Jerry hadn't seen much of each other except for their time traveling together in Sally. Wendy's quarters were in another module of the SIO, and they were both too busy with their duties for liaisons.

"Have you discovered anything new about the Dorian cube?" Wendy asked.

"No, nothing at all. It remains unopened and a complete enigma."

"What I find most exasperating," Wendy commented, "is why the Dorians would leave us a tantalizing gift within an impenetrable cube with no instructions of how to open it. When we attached golden records to each of the Voyagers, we included detailed instructions of how to play then. Why wouldn't the Dorians do the same?"

"Good question. I guess we will just have to wait until we get home and the better equipped UWSF lab can use their tools to open the cube."

Within two hours as Tesla increased it speed, Sedna shrank to the size of a beach ball.

As the days progressed, Wendy and Jerry renewed their previous liaison and began meeting daily in the observation room, usually alone. Eight days after breaking orbit, Captain Ferguson announced over the PA that VASMIR had achieved a speed of 83,600 mph. They were well on their way home, and now Sedna only appeared as a bright star in the viewing window. When Jerry signed on this expedition, he knew that a six-year absence from his family would be painful for him and for his loved ones, including his mother and father. His parents were aging and he worried about their health during his long absence, which had been even more painful for him than expected—and without the companionship of Wendy, he didn't think he could have endured it. The knowledge that he was on his way home provided comfort and quieted

88

the growing anxiety in the pit of his stomach. During this voyage, he had come to share his innermost feelings with Wendy, and told her how he felt about this long absence from his family. She sympathized but reminded him that in the days of sailing ships, such long absences as those for the crew of the HMS Beagle were routine. Yet the knowledge that others had so suffered did little to console him.

Three weeks after leaving Sedna, Wendy and Jerry met in the observation room. He used his computer to revisit some technical details of their journey home and shared them with Wendy.

"Because of the anomalies of celestial navigation and more distant swing-bye and less effective use of a gravitational assist from Neptune and Jupiter, the journey from Sedna to the moon will take longer than did the journey from the moon to Sedna. Six months after leaving Sedna, Tesla will achieve a speed of 294,600 mph and VASMIR must shut down to conserve the remaining fuel required for decelerating Tesla for moon insertion. IONISTAR will then continue to accelerate us, but even at almost 300,000 mph, our 3.5 billion mile voyage to Neptune will take twenty-six months. When we fly by Neptune, we will only be halfway home, an incredible example of the true vastness of space. Fortunately, the remaining 3.5 billion miles from Neptune to the moon will not take as long as it will take us to arrive at Neptune. Using that planet for a gravitational assist and with IONISTSAR working 24/7, we will arrive near Jupiter in six more months. When we sail past that gas giant at over 500,000 mph, the problem will be one of slowing Tesla down so it can achieve moon orbit a few months later. Tesla will use Jupiter's immense gravity to decelerate rather than accelerate us. When only ten weeks away from the moon, Tesla will rotate 180 degrees and VASMIR will use up the remaining argon fuel to decelerate Tesla for safe insertion into moon orbit. The trip from Jupiter to the moon will take five months and then thirty-eight months after leaving Sedna, we will arrive home." At least that was the plan that Jerry's computer screen displayed.

The next afternoon as Jerry visited the Command Center, a warning alarm sounded and VASMIR suddenly shut down. Those in the center scrambled to determine what had gone wrong. VASMIR had only run for twenty-six days and Jerry looked at the velocity meter. It read only 145,600 mph. Jerry watched as the crew examined their computer screens for the data that would explain why the engine had prematurely shut off.

Visibly shaken by the data, Captain Ferguson reported to all those in the room, "It appears that our main xenon fuel tank has taken a hit from a micrometer and we have lost most of our remaining fuel for IONISTAR. The same micrometer also penetrated one of our two argon tanks, leaving us with barely enough fuel in the remaining tank for VASMIR to slow Tesla down for moon insertion. To save the remaining fuel, the computer has prematurely shut VASMIR down. Without enough fuel for both IONISTAR and VASMIR, Tesla can only drift at this present speed, which will take us six-and-a-half years to arrive at Neptune, and even then, we will only be halfway home. Fortunately we can use Neptune's gravity to speed up Tesla to 254,500 mph, but even with those aids our journey from Neptune to the moon, will take another sixteen months."

The rumors of a main engine shutdown spread throughout the ship, and all on board wanted to know the details. Captain Ferguson called a meeting that night to explain what had happened.

"Folks, I have some bad news to report," he began. "As you know, the ship's VASMIR engines have prematurely shut down after only twenty-six days. Tesla collided with a small meteor, perhaps the size of a BB, but with a momentum that penetrated our fuel tanks. The meteor hit our xenon tank and one of our two argon tanks. As a result, we have lost all of our xenon for IONISTAR and two thirds of our supply of argon for VASHMIR. Unable to use those engines, we will remain at our present speed all the way to Neptune. We will use Neptune to accelerate us toward Jupiter, but even then, it will take Tesla over six and a half years to reach Neptune and then another sixteen months to arrive at the moon. We are facing an eight-year voyage home rather than a little over three years."

The news stunned Tesla's crew and passengers. A return trip of three years had now become one of eight years. In total, they would be gone from home for almost a dozen years. No one spoke for a few seconds as each person processed what this disaster would mean for him or her. Finally, Peter Ramos spoke up.

"Can't we use the remaining argon for VASMIR to accelerate us to a faster speed which would get us to Neptune in less than over six years?"

"We used VASMIR for twenty-six days after we left Sedna and consumed about a third of the fuel in the primary tank, enough to speed

Tesla up to the 145,600 mph before the engine prematurely shut down. The computer program intended Tesla to achieve a speed of 294,000 and then to shut off to conserve fuel in the remaining tank for decelerating to achieve moon orbit. The ion engine would then take over and bring us to Neptune in twenty-six months. We don't have enough argon remaining to allow us to use VASMIR to accelerate and still brake for moon insertion. In addition, we have no xenon fuel remaining for IONISTAR. We will use Neptune and Jupiter's gravity to increase our speed but we will need to conserve the remaining supply of argon. The deceleration phase must begin several weeks before we arrive at the moon; if we used a significant portion of our remaining argon now, we will not be able to decelerate Tesla for safe insertion into moon orbit. In that case we will fly right by the moon and Earth and into outer space, never to return."

"Do we have enough supplies to last eight more years?" Dr. Connie Jenkins asked.

"Yes, we have more than enough supplies to meet all our needs for a journey of even ten years. That will not be a problem."

"Aden will be twenty-four years old when I return," Jerry mumbled to Wendy.

"And I will be over fifty, single, and by then everything on Earth will have changed," she lamented as a tear ran down her cheek.

Jerry took Wendy's hand in his. "This news comes as a shock to us all, but we will be comfortable here on Tesla. Everything we knew when we left our world will be different when we get back, yet life will go on for us."

"And all our friends and relatives will have aged. I wonder if my parents will still be alive and if I will still have a job at UC Berkeley when we return," Wendy pondered.

"Each of us can continue our research careers here onboard Tesla," Jerry said. "For instance we can spend the time deciphering and using the gift in Dorian cube if we can just figure out how to open it."

Wendy smiled. "You're trying to make a silk purse out of a sow's ear."

"Perhaps, but my biggest issue right now is that this news will devastate Aden and Carol and there is no way I can to soften the blow for them," Jerry said. "Yet they had best hear it from me than from the media. My mother and father will take this news very hard."

"I will have to break the news to my mother and father as well," Wendy lamented. "They were in their late seventies when we left. I heard from my dad last week and we talked about our homecoming in just three years. Dad said Mom wasn't doing well."

Captain Ferguson and Chief Engineer Hitachi were unable to answer all the questions raised in this initial meeting, but promised another session would follow in two days, soon after he contacted UWSF and they had time to ponder alternatives.

One of those alternatives suggested by Dr. Hitachi and Dr. Marvin Thompson, the ship's navigator, involved visiting the Lassell Science and Mining station on Neptune's moon, Triton, where they could replenish their supply of xenon, argon, and supplement their supply of helium 3. The Lassell Station had the ability to extract these elements from the frozen Triton soil, and if they were able to extract enough, Tesla could immediately activate VASMIR for seventy-one days, then decelerate and arrive at Neptune in thirty-two months rather than over six years. Dr. Thompson admitted there was considerable risk in his plan. When still a long way from Neptune, they would use up all the remaining argon so that Tesla could slow down for insertion into a stable orbit around Triton. Achieving orbit around the retrograde moon was a risky maneuver that they might regret if they used all their remaining argon. Should they miss the narrow insertion window the orbit maneuver demanded, they would have no fuel remaining to make a trajectory adjustment and Tesla would either crash on Triton, Neptune, or fly off into space with no chance to return to Earth. Once in a stable Triton orbit, they could repair the damaged tanks and use the shuttle to visit the Lassell Station to obtain the necessary argon and xenon and supplement their supply of helium 3 for the return trip home. Once fully refueled, VASMIR could then accelerate Tesla to 550,000 mph and they would travel from Neptune to Jupiter in eleven months, and then use the immense gravity of Jupiter to slow Tesla down and five months later use VASMIR to slow Tesla for insertion into moon orbit. The transit time home from Neptune to the moon could be as little as sixteen months. Forty-four months travel time sounded a lot better than 108 months. Nevertheless, this plan depended on the Lassell Station's capacity to supply enough quantities of xenon and argon to refuel the ship.

Dr. Ferguson called Dr. Ed Mackey on the Lassell Station and made his request. Ed said they did not have as much argon and xenon as Tesla needed on hand, but they could speed up their mining operation and extract enough by the time Tesla arrived thirty-two months later. With that good news, Dr. Hitachi proposed that they immediately turn VASHMIR on to hasten their trip to Neptune.

Chapter Seven
Triton

Dr. Ferguson and Dr. Thompson called a meeting to explain the new travel plan. In thirty-two months, they would land on Triton where they could obtain the argon and xenon necessary to power Tesla from Triton to the moon in just sixteen months. The news that they would be arriving back on Earth in four rather than nine more years elated the crew and passengers. Dr. Thompson added a note of caution. Their computer wasn't programmed for this change of plans, nor did it include a plan to orbit Triton, a moon that rotates its host planet in an unusual retrograde orbit. It would take careful calculations and some tricky celestial navigation to park Tesla in a stable orbit around Triton, and there was a small chance that this maneuver would not be successful. In that case, they might go flying off into space or crash on Triton. Excited about the possibility of a shortened trip, most folks ignored Dr. Thompson's cautionary warnings, but not Jerry who fully understood the dangers of this risky maneuver. He studied Dr. Thompson's math, and although he didn't find fault with it, the narrow portal insertion window deeply concerned him. Even a .01 percent velocity error or 0.5-degree insertion angle error would result in either skipping past Triton or crashing into it. To commit to a landing on Triton, in just a few months they would have to rotate and use all their remaining argon to slow down. Without any fuel remaining and should they miss the portal window, they could fly off into space without the ability to correct their trajectory. They could go drifting off into space forever, never to return to Earth. He shared his misgivings privately with Dr. Thompson.

Marvin was defensive. "Yes, it is true there is some danger of flying off into space or crashing into Triton, but what would you suggest we do—continue our nine-year journey home?"

Jerry had to admit the prospect of a nine-year voyage was unacceptable to not only the officers, crew, and passengers onboard Tesla, but also to the UWSF managers who had discussed, reviewed, and approved Dr. Thompson's plan. In addition, there was a silk lining in the plan to visit Triton. Dr. Mackey's laboratory was the best-outfitted metrology lab outside Earth. Jerry and the other scientists had been unable to find a way inside the Dorian cube, but perhaps with the analytical equipment in the Lassell Station labs, they could do so.

Despite Jerry's concern, it was time to put the Triton plan into action. Marvin activated VASMIR and seventy-one days later Tesla achieved maximum speed. A few months after that, Tesla rotated and VASMIR began breaking for insertion into orbit around Triton, which on arrival must exactly match Triton's retrograde orbital speed.

****

October 2123

In the observation room, with Dr. Thompson and other Tesla crewmembers, Jerry and Wendy watched as Neptune grew to the size of a blue-green beach ball and Triton to the size and color of an orange.

"This is going to be an exacting orbital insertion," Marvin admitted. "Neptune's strong gravity is trying to force us to orbit around it, but with VASMIR's help we will direct Tesla into a retrograde insertion orbit around Triton." "Little Blue," Marvin's nickname for the Tesla navigation computer, "will be up to the job." Jerry and Marvin then went to join Dr. Ferguson and the other officers in the Control Room to monitor the insertion program and watch as Little Blue nudged Tesla into the narrow insertion window.

No one noticed Marvin's presence as he entered the Control Room and sat down at his station.

As they closed in on Triton, the moon grew in size until it filled the main Control Room view screen, yet Jerry noticed that no one was watching that screen. All eyes remained glued to the graphical navigation screen that depicted the narrow insertion window Tesla must enter and the critical velocity for a successful orbit around Triton. A red X marked Tesla's present position, and the velocity showed up numerically below the slowly moving X. A yellow line extending beyond the X marked Tesla's projected trajectory based on its present position and velocity, and two dashed red curves on either side represented the maximum allowable deviation from the yellow line that Tesla must follow to enter the insertion window. Everyone held their breath and watched as the X inched along the yellow line and approached the mouth of the insertion window. Big Blue was doing a fantastic job navigating Tesla into the window, but Dr. Thompson sat at the control panel ready to make manual corrections to their velocity and trajectory should it become necessary. As they watched, the X and yellow line began to drift toward one red line. At first, the deviation was barely noticeable, but soon it was clear the X and the predicted yellow path would miss the window. Big Blue was experiencing an anomaly not expected in the trajectory program.

"We are encountering an unexpected gravitational anomaly on Triton and if not corrected we will miss the window," Dr. Thompson commented. "I am making manual corrections."

Gradually the X began to drift back and the yellow line predicted a safe entry as Tesla approached the window. Tesla slipped inside the window and three minutes later emerged in a circular orbit 235 miles above Triton's surface. Everyone let out a collective sigh and then cheered when Dr. Thompson announced that Tesla had achieved a stable orbit above the moon's surface. Dr. Ferguson relayed the message to the Tesla passengers and crew over the intercom.

Locked in a synchronous orbit 354,000 km above Neptune, Triton revolved and rotated in a little less than six days, always presenting the same face toward its host planet. The Lassell Station sat within the 50-mile wide Hubble Crater. As Tesla flew over the Hubble Crater on its first orbit, Dr. Ferguson contacted Dr. Ed Mackey at the Lassell Station and announced their successful insertion into orbit about Triton.

"Congratulations. I know that this was not an easy insertion for Tesla," Ed said, "and it is good to know that you are all safe. However, I have some disturbing news for you. We have been hard at work for thirty-two months extracting argon and xenon to meet your needs, but at this point we have only two-thirds of argon necessary for your successful return trip to the Moon. Tesla's sister ship, Michelson, will arrive here in nine months and we must extract enough argon for their return trip. We estimate it will take another three months to extract a sufficient amount of argon for Tesla and still have enough to fuel Michelson when it arrives."

"That is disappointing news, Ed," Dr. Ferguson lamented. "I suppose we can remain in orbit around Triton indefinitely, but the crew trusted that we would be on our way to the moon by next week. Is there anything Tesla can do to help speed up the argon recovery process?"

"Unfortunately I don't think there is anything you can do to speed up recovery. However, we would welcome a visit by you and your crew. Our principal scientist and amateur paleontologist, Dr. Laura Pavli, is most eager to meet Dr. Jerry Abrams and examine the bone he found on Sedna in her fully equipped lab. In addition, I am eager to examine the Dorian cube. Can you bring it with you? I understand that you have had no luck opening it. Perhaps our laboratory could help."

"Dr. Abram and I with some other Tesla folks plan to take the shuttle to the surface the day after tomorrow." Then with a nod to Jerry, he added, "You can tell Dr. Pavli that Dr. Abrams will bring the fossil and the Dorian cube with him."

Communication between Tesla and Lassell Station could only take place for the few minutes that Tesla passed between Neptune and Triton where that moon wouldn't block their signal. They were about to be out of range.

Dr. Mackey ended the transmission with, "We will be looking forward to meeting with you and your team on Wednesday."

On subsequent orbits around Triton, Jerry and Wendy viewed the moon's surface from their 235-mile-high orbit. The complex salmon-colored ground pockmarked by circular depressions looked like the surface of a cantaloupe. These were not impact craters as one might assume, but collapsed surface regions each roughly the same size. The few true impact craters in the mottled surface were filled to the brim with water and nitrogen ices. Smooth pink ice caps covered both poles, and one section on the northeast corner of the far side sported a rugged glacial mountain range three thousand meters high. The limb of the moon revealed a tenuous fuzzy gas atmosphere of sublimated methane and nitrogen ice.

Amid groans from his Tesla audience, Dr. Ferguson explained the three-month delay. After the early excitement engendered by the news that they could be home in another few months, another twelve-week delay was almost unbearable.

"Is there anything we can do to speed up the extraction process?" Bill Summerset asked.

"Dr. Mackey doesn't think so, although perhaps with your metallurgical experience you could help them at the Lassell Station."

Bill agreed go with them to the surface.

Wednesday morning, Tesla's chief engineer Dr. Hitachi and Tesla's information officer Gina Tappan joined Bill, Jerry, and Dr. Mitera as Dr. Vincent prepared for the shuttle ride to Lassell Station. Jerry carried the fossil in a vial in his pocket and the cube in the transit box stowed inside his backpack. As the team gathered in the hangar, technicians were fueling and making last-minute shuttle preparations. After the shuttle launched, it made four spiraling revolutions around Triton and then when only 5 miles above the surface, the onboard computer locked onto the Lassell station homing beacon; ten minutes later the shuttle connected with the station's main air lock.

Dr. Mackey, Dr. Bernadette "Bernie" Cary the resident astrophysicist, and Dr. Ann Pavli were the first in line to greet Dr. Vincent and his team. Dr. Mackey introduced Dr. Cary, and then Dr. Pavli, the station's principal scientist, and finally the other staff scientists. As Jerry shook hands with Ann, her personal warmth and charm embraced him. He returned her warmhearted smile. Ann then led them to the conference room where Bernie presented a slide show about the Lassell Station. The Lassell folks wanted to hear all about Sedna, the fossil, and most of all the Dorian archives and the Dorian cube, but Dr. Mackey asked them to hold their questions until as a good host he took the Tesla folks on a tour of the station. Gina and Jerry promised they would hold a briefing session later that evening and give out details about their Sedna discoveries. Dr. Mackey, Bernie, and Ann then took the Tesla folks on the promised tour of the station. Dr. Mackey's metrology lab impressed Jerry. No lab outside Earth was better equipped with the latest qualitative and quantitative analytical equipment than the Lassell metrology lab. Jerry thought it would be an excellent place to learn more about the cube.

As Ann led them out of the metrology lab, she excused herself. "Dr. Mackey and Bernie will continue the tour to the gasification factory. I will meet you back here afterwards."

The gasification factory was located a mile away from the Station. It was surrounded by a dozen three-story-high cylindrical storage silos and powered by a fusion reactor. The 200-foot diameter domed plant separated the various gasses by heating the Triton regolith. Dr. Mackey and Bernie led Jerry, Bill, and Dr. Mitera into the gasification factory where they could observe the separation process for obtaining and purifying Triton surface materials including oxygen, nitrogen, xenon, argon, and helium 3.

"Triton is a treasure trove of materials," Bernie explained. "Almost every element in the periodic table exists in the soil, rocks, and ices of this moon. We are mining helium 3, iridium, and several other rare earth elements that are scarce on Earth but plentiful here on Triton. We have three tractor-trucks that transport material from our primary mining site lying about five miles from here to the plant. The trucks bring the mined material into the factory via an air lock and deposit them into large storage bins. The material is then crushed, sifted, and finally heated at various temperatures to extract the many valuable materials needed on Earth. The extraction process also produces all the oxygen, water, and other materials required for the Station. The argon and xenon you need for Tesla is a by-product of our helium 3 extraction process. It is so cold on Triton that argon, which freezes at 308 degrees Fahrenheit below zero, is a solid."

Dr. Mackey explained why it would take them so long to extract the argon for Tesla's return trip. "It takes two tons of surface regolith and four hours of processing to produce just ten liters of argon and three liters of xenon, so you can see why it will take three more months to obtain the 5,500 liters of argon that you require for your trip home. We already have the 2,200 liters of xenon you asked for, so it is not a problem. To produce enough power to run the factory and the Lassell Station, we have two helium 3 fusion reactors similar to the one on Tesla. Every two years our supply ship, the Michelson, makes the two-year journey to Triton. It will arrive here in nine months and then we will load the rare mineral products of our mining operation and hundreds of liters of helium 3, and then refuel their ship with argon and xenon necessary for their return trip."

When Jerry returned from the tour, Dr. Pavli who had been waiting for him outside her office greeted him with a friendly smile. Ann's warmth had impressed Jerry the minute they first shook hands. She was intelligent, personable, and charming. Despite her obvious excitement to have a look at the Sedna fossil and the cube, she did not allow her impatience to cut short a proper welcome and instead greeted Jerry with a hug.

"Glad to see you again," she said, "and I hope you enjoyed the tour."

"I most certainly did," Jerry said.

"I assume you have the fossil and cube with you," she said.

"Yes, I do," Jerry admitted.

"You can give the cube to our lab scientists for analysis," Ann suggested.

"The cube is in my backpack, and I am charged not to let it out of my sight. I hope you don't mind if your scientists only examine it in my presence."

"I understand; bring the cube with you into the metrology lab and I'll have our scientists meet us there," she said. "But first I would like to have a look at the fossil."

Ann took Jerry by the hand and led him down the hall into her well-equipped metrology laboratory. Jerry again marveled at the latest analytical and metrology equipment in the lab, from a laser mass spectrometer to electron and neutron microscopes.

Jerry took the vial out of his pocket and handed it to Ann. She turned the vial around and around under the bright lights of an examination table.

"Tell me again how you found this fossil."

"We were digging a hole in the Walnut Valley on Sedna to place explosives and a seismometer to study the subsurface, and as the auger bought up material from a depth of about three meters, I noticed an unusual rock with a pale yellow rod protruding from one end. When I removed the crumbly rock surrounding the rod, to me it looked like a fossil.

"Did you find any other bones or unusual rocks when digging around?"

"No. I carefully sifted through the rest of the pile of material, but this was the only unusual rock that I found. However, on a subsequent exploration of the Valley we did find some other possible fossils in the same depression."

"May I remove the fossil from the vial?" Jerry gave Ann permission and she took the fossil out of the vial and placed it under an ancient stereo microscope.

Jerry smiled and commented, "With all the high-tech equipment in your lab, you still use a twentieth century microscope?"

"Even though it is over 200 years old, this microscope is my most trusted piece of equipment. Those Zeiss folks knew how to make first-class optical instruments."

After a few seconds, Ann looked away from the microscope. "There is no doubt in my mind that this is fossilized bone; a bone that once belonged to a mammal. It is a malleus or hammer, which is part of the middle ear and the smallest bone in the body. However, this particular malleus is much larger than any belonging to mammals as small as humans. This mammal must have been as large as a horse."

"It is mind-blowing that we would have discovered this fossil while just randomly digging two holes in the valley floor, but perhaps it was not all that random. We selected this particular spot to locate our seismometer because it was an unusual depression in the otherwise flat valley floor, and could have been the site of an ancient lake," Jerry explained. "Although later on we found additional samples at the same location, we were unable to find any fossils elsewhere on Sedna"

Ann nodded her understanding. "Random or not, despite many searches throughout our solar system for evidence of life, we have not discovered any creatures dead or alive other than extinct early microbe exoskeletons and microorganisms surviving underground on Mars. Some folks argue that this is an example of panspermia—in other words that these Mars microbes actually came from Earth and did not independently arise on Mars. Yet Sedna is so remote the odds of contamination from Earth are zero. This is such an important discovery that it almost eclipses your discovery of the door."

"Well, paleontology was not our mission, nor are we educated as paleontologists. Such an expedition will have to wait for a dedicated UWSF team, and rest assured there will be one."

Ann then placed the bone in her analyzer. The printout showed that it was made of silicates.

"You said a subterranean layer of water exists in Walnut Valley. This makes sense because for silicates to replace the calcium in a bone, there had to be surface water in the past."

Dr. Mackey and Dr. Vincent joined Ann, and Jerry and Ann explained the bone came from the inner ear of a mammal.

This amazed Dr. Mackey. "You mean to tell me that Jerry discovered a fossilized mammalian bone on Sedna?"

"That is exactly what I am saying," Ann said with conviction, "and it is a bone from a large mammal, perhaps the size of a horse."

"This is astounding. Are you sure it belonged to a mammal?" Dr. Mackey asked to confirm.

"I'm positive," she said.

"Other than a few microbes on Mars, this is the first evidence of independent life beyond Earth, and who would think that this discovery would be on an out-of-the-way ice rock such as Sedna. We will have to contact UWSF and report that we have confirmed the Sedna fossil once belonged to a mammal," Dr. Mackey said.

Ann agreed to do so. The other Lassell scientists who were eager to examine the cube soon joined Dr. Mackey, Josh, Ann, and Jerry in the lab. Jerry took off his backpack, extracted the cube from the transit box, and handed it to Dr. Mackey.

He turned it repeatedly in his hands and then said, "The cube is slightly warm to the touch and as black as black can be. Although highly polished, it does not reflect incident light." He then gave it to Ann who placed it in the X-ray Lithochemistry and Nuclear Magnetic Resonance analyzers.

After a brief examination Ann reported, "The material in the cube has such a low reflectivity or albedo, as close to zero as possible, that it is hard to get a quantitative reading of the elements that make up this device. Except for a 7 cm diameter sphere in the center of the cube, it is solid and consists of a crystalline metal that behaves like a single molecule. Our instrument detected iron, carbon, titanium, cobalt, and a surprising amount of thulium, a rare element on earth. The sphere contains a crystalline form of stainless steel."

They tried to cut into the cube, but no technology available in the Lassell Station could penetrate or even scratch it.

After several attempts, Ann said, "I'm sorry but we cannot help you get inside the cube. Perhaps the tools at the UWSF labs back on earth can do so. They claim they can nondestructively cut into anything."

Further examinations produced no more information about the cube except to confirm what Dr. Vincent's team had previously discovered.

Despite disappointment, they ended the examination and Jerry returned the cube to the container and his backpack.

Dr. Mackey then said to Jerry, "Tomorrow Bernie and I are taking Bill Summerset to visit our mine and thought you and some of the team might like to come along to see 'Old Faithful.'"

"Old Faithful?" Jerry asked.

"Yes, that is what we call an ice volcano that erupts every ten days, just like clockwork. It is due to erupt at 10:35 tomorrow morning."

Early the next morning, Jerry, Bill, and Gina joined Dr. Mackey, Ann Pavli, Bernie, and the tractor driver, Paul Hancock, in the hangar. Dr. Hitachi volunteered to remain at the station to help diagnose a technical problem with the Lassell fusion reactor.

Paul told his passengers to don space suits, complete except for helmets. This was the standard practice for travel on the surface of Triton. They dressed, climbed aboard the passenger tractor, and then drove out onto the flat regolith and ice-covered plain that covered the Hubble Crater floor.

"This 'ice' is a mixture of water, ammonia, methane, and nitrogen ice," Bernie explained. "The surface of Triton is 391 degrees Fahrenheit below zero, the coldest place in the solar system. All gasses freeze at this temperature, yet below the ice-covered surface is an ocean of liquid water, methane, and ammonia. Neptune's gravity pulls and squeezes Triton in its six-hour stretched orbit around the planet, raising tides that heat the ice and maintain a liquid ocean about 2 miles deep. Internal pressure forces the liquid to the surface through cracks where it erupts as cyrovolcanoes."

The volcano lay 15 miles away and after one hour of winding between small hillocks of ice and crossing over wide crevasses on ice bridges, Bernie announced that they had arrived. Jerry expected to see a cone or small mound that would mark the volcano, but when the tractor stopped on top of a small hill, there was nothing to see in the distance except a long jagged crevasse—a crack in the surface several meters wide surrounded by mounds of ice.

"Where's the volcano?" Jerry asked.

"Right over there," Paul said, pointing to the crevasse that was 500 yards away. "We have to stay well back of that crack," he warned. He looked at his watch and then added, "It will erupt any minute now."

As predicted, few minutes later the ground began to shake and a small geyser erupted from the crack, spewing a fountain of liquid to a height of several feet, and then dwindled and fell back into the crack.

"That's it?" Gina asked, audibly disappointed.

"Just wait … that was only foreplay," Ann explained.

The geyser returned in every increasing burps, belching a fountain that grew higher and higher with each eruption until a column of water, methane, and ammonia two meters wide thrust itself high into the sky.

Jerry craned his neck to see the top of the fountain, but it was already too high to be visible. Ammonia and nitrogen snow and three-inch diameter balls of water ice began to fall in slow motion from the top of the fountain. On impact with the ground, the ice balls shattered into shards, while the more slowly falling nitrogen snow draped the mounds on either side of the crevasse. The eruption continued for ten full minutes until the column gradually decreased and finally collapsed back into the depths of the crevasse. In the weak gravity, a shower of ice balls and nitrogen snow continued to fall long after the geyser disappeared.

"That was quite a show," Bill commented.

"There are dozens of other ice volcanoes in the area, some even larger than Old Faithful, but none erupt on a schedule such as this one does," Dr. Markey explained.

"It's time to visit the mine," Bernie suggested.

They traveled another eight miles over fields and mounds of tortured ice, crossing over meter-wide cracks that cut across the landscape in jagged streaks. When Paul came to one wide enough to qualify as a crevasse, he slowed down and searched for a snow bridge where the tractor could safely cross over.

"We have to be careful when crossing over these crevasses," Paul warned. "The snow bridges can be deceptively fragile. Some of them that at first glance look strong are anything but. In fact we lost a tractor in one two months ago." He said this as they crossed over a snow bridge about five meters wide.

"What happened to the crew in that tractor?" Bill asked.

"When the tractor was just a few feet along on the bridge," Paul answered, "the whole suspension began to shudder. The driver stopped the tractor and ordered everyone to put on his or her helmets and then climb out and cross over the bridge to solid ground. When everyone was clear, the driver tried to back the tractor off, but when it moved big chunks of the bridge began to crack and break off. Thankfully, the driver had time to get out before the bridge and tractor disappeared into the abyss. "Now you know why I made everyone climb into full space suits," Paul explained.

Bill shuddered and glanced into the black depth of the crevasses as they crossed on the snow bridge. If the chasm had a bottom, it wasn't visible. "Were you able to recover the tractor?" He asked.

"No, we were not," Paul admitted. "The tractor still rests at the bottom of the crevasse. No one knows how deep that abyss is."

Picking their way around any crevasse too wide for the tractor to cross over or without a solid ice bridge, they came to a 15-meter wide crevasse obviously much too wide to cross over. They followed this crevasse for over a mile until they came to an aluminum bridge that spanned the wide crevasse.

"Because this crevasse continues for fifteen miles in either direction, we erected this bridge so the trucks could have a shortcut to the factory," Paul explained.

"How deep is this chasm?" Bill asked as they crossed over.

"We don't know," he answered. "As far as we can tell, it's bottomless."

A half hour later, they arrived at the mine entrance, a 10-meter wide cave blasted into the side of a glacial cliff several hundred meters high.

The tractor entered the cave, passed through an air lock, and then drove down a long tunnel that emptied into an enormous, dimly lit cavern. Jerry had visited ice caverns before, but this one took his breath away. The walls and ceiling glowed translucent blue and were covered by tiny ice crystals that sparkled in the faint light. As vehicle headlights played across the cave, rhombic thumb-size ice prisms that jutted from the walls painted the cavern with rainbows of shimmering light patterns that danced across the walls and ceiling. He had never before seen any cave so beautiful or more splendidly arrayed. As they climbed out of the tractor, warm filtered air tainted with a slight hint of pungent dust filled their lungs. Several minors clothed only in light work coveralls and wearing lighted helmets scurried about the cavern as they performed their various duties. A machine chewed away at one far wall where a conveyor belt carried the extracted rocks across the cave and dumped them into a waiting tractor bed. Ann picked up two fist-sized rocks from the conveyor belt and handed one to Jerry and another to Bill. The rocks, heavy and as cold as dry ice, were a conglomerate of dark rock streaked with bands of white material. Without protective gloves, those rocks would freeze their hands.

"There are more minerals in those hunks of frozen rock than you can imagine," Ann claimed. "They contain iridium, manganese, molybdenum, copper, silver, gold, and platinum to name just a few elements. We get water, helium 3, oxygen, nitrogen, your precious argon and xenon, and other minerals and gasses by crushing and heating these conglomerated rocks and surface regolith."

After a short tour of the cavern, Dr. Mackey hinted that it was time to return to the Lassell Station. They all piled back inside the tractor, and as it began the journey back to the station, Ann explained why Triton was so rich in elements from the periodic table.

"It is interesting that all the heavier materials mined on Earth come from asteroids that bombarded the surface eons ago," she said. "All the heavier elements including iron in the early molten Earth sank to the core, leaving the surface mostly lacking in heavy metals. Although Triton has a semisolid core and had a molten past, this moon solidified before the heavier elements had a chance to sink to the core, leaving a plethora of heavy metals on the surface where they can be easily mined."

Bill, who had remained unusually quiet during Ann's explanation, finally spoke up.

"The origin of the rare elements that you are mining on Triton is complex and there is a good reason why elements heavier than iron are rare. The periodic table of elements heavier than iron were not formed by nuclear fusion as is iron and everything lighter than iron, but were formed by neutron bombardment originating in supernovas. Before each supernova exploded, the dying star ejected iron and other lighter elements, which then gathered in a surrounding nebula. When the supernova exploded, neutrons and gamma rays bombarded those elements and created a long list of heavy elements and their isotopes. When bombarded by gamma rays, some of the neutrons in these isotopes change to protons and form elements heavier than iron. Copper for example forms when three of the neutrons in iron (26 protons and 30 neutrons) emit an electron and become protons to form a nucleus consisting of 29 protons. This process of neutron bombardment and decay continues to form each of the other elements in the Periodic Table up to the element zirconium. Yet even a supernova is not energetic enough to form heavier elements such as iridium, silver, gold, lead, and uranium. Those elements require more energy than a normal supernova can produce. The heaviest elements only form in hypernovas that exploded by the merger of two neutron stars. All the gold and silver in your rings and the iridium, rare earths, and uranium mined here and on Earth were formed by neutron bombardment and the decay that originated in neutron star hypernova explosions."

Bernie was absentmindedly rotating her gold wedding ring as Bill spoke. "Yes, this is true," she said. "It is also interesting that most radioactive elements on Triton such as uranium and thorium are not present in any abundance on the surface but sank to the core early in the moon's history, before the core solidified. Although the gravitational action from Neptune contributes to heat Triton's subsurface, radioactive decay is largely responsible for our liquid ocean and ice volcanoes."

"We think the same process may have also occurred on Sedna," Bill added. "Our geological expedition discovered radioactive materials that melted the core and heated an ocean of water-methane slush."

"Yes, but your geological findings were far from the most interesting discovery you made while on Sedna," Bernie said. "Please, tell us about the Dorian archives."

"As we promised, we will have a debriefing for everyone tonight," Gina reminded her.

Later that evening as promised, Jerry and Dr. Vincent presented the folks at Lassell Station with a brief summary of their expedition on Sedna and their discovery of the archives. Since many of the scientists at Lassell were geologists, Jerry spent most of his time talking about the geology of Sedna.

Dr. Vincent ended the presentation by saying, "After traveling from their home for several generations, the Dorians finally arrived on Earth roughly sixty-five million years ago. Their goal was to reestablish their civilization, but because the Earth had been devastated by a collision with an asteroid, it was impossible for them to prosper there. The inability to thrive forced them to leave. Before they traveled beyond our solar system, they set up the time capsule on Sedna and left a gift protected by this cube for the beings they assumed would someday visit. They placed their legacy at the outer limits of our solar system so only when an intelligent species could travel in space and find the Dorian gift would they be capable of using it. Unfortunately we have not yet been able to open the cube, so we can only surmise what the Dorian gift may be. Perhaps the UWSF labs back on Earth have the technology to open the cube. Hopefully the Dorians finally arrived on their new world and today their civilization is thriving. Although unlikely, perhaps someday we will meet them."

After the lecture ended, Ann invited Jerry to have dinner alone with her in her apartment. As they sat together eating and enjoying each other's company, Ann shared her thoughts about the cube.

"I have been pondering why the Dorians encased their gift in a cube that we cannot open with our technology. This doesn't make sense to me."

Jerry thought for a moment and answered, "They designed the cube as a container to protect their gift. They made it robust so it would endure the millions of years it would take before discovery. Perhaps they assumed we would have better technology than we now do."

Jerry's explanation didn't convince her, but she let the question remain unanswered. The next day, Dr. Hitachi, Gina Tappan, Jerry, Dr. Mitera, Bill Summerset, and Dr. Vincent said good-bye to their hosts, climbed aboard the shuttle, and returned to Tesla.

After they arrived, Jerry met privately with Dr. Vincent and shared Ann's concern about the cube's design that didn't allow them to open it. Josh dismissed her apprehension by saying the Dorians had made the cube robust to survive the intervening millions of years while it waited for discovery.

"They have left us something wonderful inside that cube," Josh argued, "and back on Earth, the USWF lab has the means to open the cube and extract the Dorian gift. We must be patient and wait until that time."

During the next few weeks, almost all the passengers aboard Tesla visited the Lassell Station, and many of the Lassell folks visited Tesla. By November 6, 2124, the Lassell miners had extracted and processed enough argon and xenon for the trip home. They made a final transmission to the folks on Lassell as Dr. Thompson activated his navigation program. Dr. Hitachi started VASMIR and began their sixteen-month trip back to Earth. Twenty days later, Tesla had sped up to over 100,000mph.

Jerry and Wendy resumed their daily visit to the observation room. On the return trip, they passed within a million miles of cloud-shrouded Triton where the UWSF had established a domed research station at the edge of a northern methane sea. As they passed Saturn, they admired the beautiful rings and the swirling bands of gas around the planet and the exquisite aura on Saturn's poles.

"Hands down Saturn must be the most beautiful sight in the solar system," Wendy said.

Jerry disagreed. "Look just to the left of the rings and you will see a little blue dot. That little dot is Earth, and for me that is the most beautiful sight in the solar system." Wendy could only agree.

Chapter Eight
Mars Calls

September 2124

Nine months after leaving Triton, Tesla had increased its speed to 550,000 mph and now they were four months from a rendezvous with Jupiter. When they arrived, they would use that huge planet's gravity to decrease their speed to 330,000 mph to prepare for further breaking and insertion into orbit about the moon. As they swung around Jupiter, its huge bulk filled the observation room window. Dozens of passengers crowded into the room with Jerry and Wendy and marveled at the sight only a few thousand miles below. Gigantic hurricanes the size of Earth floated across the planet's surface, chaperoned by the bands of wind-driven atmosphere, each belt arrayed in various shades of pink, red, umber, and blue. The giant red spot remained impressive although decreased from its former size when discovered centuries ago. The close approach lasted 10 minutes, presenting brilliant views of the auras that hovered over both poles. As Tesla sped past Jupiter and toward home, one by one folks exited the observation room until Jerry and Wendy were once again alone and stayed on for four hours to view Ganymede as Tesla passed only fifteen thousand miles above that moon's frozen surface. Jerry searched the surface through the lounge's telescope.

"Ganymede is the largest moon in the solar system, larger than either Mercury or Pluto, and only slightly smaller than Mars," Jerry said. "The project on Ganymede ended twelve years ago in a big disappointment for the UWSF folks who invested years of time and money to find life presumed to exist in its subterranean oceans. I can see the remnants of the domes they built dedicated to drilling through the miles of ice to the ocean beneath, where most scientists insisted life swam, but it didn't. Mechanized submarines searched for many months, yet they never found evidence of life. All the ingredients for life existed in that global ocean, a cauldron of life-forming chemicals and organics that somehow failed to even produce a primitive microbe."

"Obviously life is atypical, at least in this solar system," Wendy said. "As far as our research can determine, only Earth and Mars have evolved living organisms, and then it is unclear if these examples of life which share similar DNA evolved independently or was transferred between the two planets."

Tesla would cross Mar's orbit some distance from that planet and in the mostly empty space between Jupiter and Earth, there was little in the observation lounge to capture their interest. As a result, Jerry and Wendy began to spend more of their free time together in the holographic entertainment room on deck two. Because of the high demand for the entertainment room, they had to sign up for time slots well in advance, which limited their visits to three or four hours a week. The holographic program engaged all five senses of the observer to create a realistic experience. It was a marvel of twenty-second century entertainment. Wendy's favorite program was a visit to a sandy beach in Hawaii, and for Jerry a walk through a Redwood forest in California. Wendy's seaside program projected an Oahu beach in full sensory realism. They could hear the roar of waves that rhythmically crashed on the beach, feel the warmth of the sun on their bodies, the caress of a gentle breeze on their cheeks, the fragrance of the ocean and the taste of its salty air. They watched pelicans fly in single formation up and down the beach and sandpipers dance in the retreating surf as they searched for a meal. It was as real as if they were there.

Holding hands, they usually sat quietly together on a dune just enjoying the scene and drinking in the peacefulness that enfolded them. Raptured by the experience, Wendy used a particular occasion to ponder the immensity of the universe. She picked up a fistful of dry sand and let it sift slowly between her fingers.

"Jerry, if you could imagine that each grain of sand in my hand represents a sun, then perhaps my hand can hold a few hundred thousand of them. Look up and down this beach as far as the hologram projects, and imagine how many billion handfuls of suns are on this beach, yet all the sand on this beach does not begin to account for the number of suns in the universe. One would have to include not only all the sand on this beach but on all the other beaches on Earth to come close to a true count. The numbers are incomprehensible."

"That analogy helps me picture such huge numbers," Jerry responded. "But what is your point?"

"We now know that we are not alone. For centuries, skeptical scientists have argued that if aliens exist and have visited Earth, then where are they, then and now? Many have inferred that without such physical evidence, then indeed, we are most probably alone. Now we have discovered such evidence and have destroyed their argument that humans are the only sentient beings in this vast universe. Yet, even before our discovery on Sedna, the argument for other sentient beings was irrefutable. Out there in all the immensity of creation, statistically we cannot be the only intelligent beings in existence. Assume that in a dozen handfuls of sand there is only one grain with an environment that allows sentient beings to evolve. Then there must be untold numbers of alien races thriving throughout the universe yet we have evidence of only one."

"True, but these countless suns are spaced so far apart from one another that an encounter between aliens must be a rare event. It took centuries and generations of Dorians for them to travel here, and that onetime visit occurred over sixty million years before humans ever evolved."

Wendy smiled. "The cube is proof that space-faring beings existed long before humanity evolved on Earth and that we humans are late bloomers, early in our evolutionary timetable. Our visit to Sedna was a historic moment for our species, and one that I am proud to have witnessed. We proved beyond any doubt that humans are indeed not alone and life is ubiquitous."

Jerry squeezed Wendy's hand even tighter.

"This realization makes all humanity seem insignificant and unexciting, an emerging child of the universe. First we discovered that we are not the center of the universe, and then we learned that we are not even the center of the solar system. Now we know that we are not the center of creation. I wonder how those folks back on Earth who think otherwise will adjust to this latest news."

****

Two weeks after Tesla's rendezvous with Jupiter and its moons, an urgent call for Captain Jack Ferguson arrived in the control room. The call was from Dr. Sera Lindgren, the director of the Martian Terraforming Project (MTFP) and a longtime friend of Josh Vincent.

As a part of the feasibility study for the Mars Terraforming Project, twenty years ago the MTFP built its first fusion reactor and gas conversion factory at the Bonestell Crater found on the Mare Acidalium quadrangle situated on the Acidalia Planitia of Mars. The project's first objective was to demonstrate that they could thermally melt subsurface permafrost and fill the crater with melt-water. At the same time, the factory released copious amounts of CO_2 and nitrogen gas into the Martian atmosphere. The initial results were impressive and, after twenty years, the factory had increased the measurable amount of CO_2 and nitrogen in the Martian atmosphere by 12 percent and raised the surface air pressure by 5 percent. Water now filled the Bonestell Crater to a depth of 466 feet. Other CO_2 and nitrogen factories were on the drawing board, and the second of a dozen planned factories was almost on line. In ten years, factories across the surface of the planet would be melting water and releasing gasses. The subsequent greenhouse effect will warm the Martian atmosphere to above freezing and melt much of the subsurface permafrost to form lakes all across the surface of Mars. In phase three, the project will introduce blue-green alga into the lakes, and the resulting photosynthesis will release oxygen into the atmosphere. Eventually, perhaps in two or three hundred years, Mars will have a sustainable and breathable atmosphere. This ambitious effort had now completed phase-one and started phase-two of a project that would take over 120 years to complete, yet they had successfully demonstrated the Mars Terraforming Project was viable.

Sera explained that a hydrogen explosion in the factory building designed to extract helium 3 from Mars soils had damaged the reactor and the gasification factory, and destroyed their stored supply of helium 3 that powered the fusion reactor. Without this fuel and fusion reactor, their terraforming project would come to a grinding halt. They desperately needed the extra helium 3 onboard Tesla and the help of Tesla reactor technicians to repair the MTFP extraction factory.

Although Tesla was still three months away from crossing Mars' orbit, it was the only starship in the vicinity. Tesla's sister ship Michelson which also serviced the MTFP was already outbound and well beyond Saturn on the way to service the Lassell Station on Triton. Dr. Lindgren was asking Tesla to make an unscheduled rendezvous with Mars, and then send down a shuttle with the required reactor fuels. She also requested that because the reactor explosion had killed two fusion reactor technicians, they also needed reactor technicians to help repair the reactor and gasification factory. She was aware that Tesla had on board an extra supply of helium 3, spare reactor parts, and a team of qualified reactor technicians. She needed all three items.

Captain Ferguson responded. "You must understand that we have precious cargo on board, and the UWSF managers are eager to have the Dorian cube in their hands. I doubt that they will agree to divert Tesla to Mars, which would delay our arrival home by several months. Nevertheless, I will contact the UWSF managers for instructions. Should they approve this unscheduled mission, navigator Thompson will have to solve several navigational problems. The biggest is that after leaving Jupiter, the ship is now traveling over 360,000 mph and to slow down for an intercept with Mars, we will have to start applying the brakes immediately and do so for another three months. The trip from Jupiter to Mars will take eight months, delay our arrival back home, and will force us to use our reserve of argon, leaving just enough left to brake for insertion into moon orbit. Our present trajectory to the moon takes us some distance from the red planet, so navigator Thompson will have to plot a new navigational trajectory, one that will allow us to slow down and rendezvous with the red planet. This delay to our eventual homecoming will be unpopular with the passengers and crew."

"I understand, but our need is critical," Sera countered. "Please contact UWSF with my proposal as soon as possible."

Unexpectedly, the UWSF managers readily approved the Tesla mission to Mars. Captain Ferguson knew that those on Tesla would loathe another unscheduled delay, but they must understand how critical this change in plans was for the success of the MTFP and the terraforming project on Mars. In a community meeting that evening, Captain Ferguson and Dr. Vincent announced the UWSF had ordered Tesla to Mars to help the MTFP bring their fusion reactor on line. He tried to explain why this change in plans was necessary.

As expected, such news angered the passengers and crew.

"How many months will this delay cause?" Peter asked.

Dr. Thompson estimated that this mission to Mars would delay their arrival home by at least eight months and any time spent on Mars. The auditorium erupted in a combined painful moan. Folks had been counting the days remaining until they arrived home, and now with another delay the voyage home would be months longer. Nevertheless, orders were orders and no one expected Captain Ferguson to argue with the UWSF managers about the change of plans.

****

May 2125

Dr. Thompson's recomputed trajectory had slowed Tesla enough to ease into a circular orbit 1,875 miles above Mars. The away team including chief engineer Dr. Hitachi, Dr. Vincent, Jerry, Bill Summerset, Gina Tappan, and Dr. Mitera, and with three reactor technicians prepared to board the shuttle for the trip to the surface. Dr. Vincent told Jerry that he did not want him to take the cube to the surface and directed him to place the cube and fossils in the care of Dr. Ferguson while he was on Mars. Jerry kept the original fossil with him so he could show it to the folks on Mars.

Since the shuttle used argon to fuel the small onboard VASMIR engine, and Tesla had little argon to spare, the shuttle could only make one round trip to the surface of Mars. They loaded the passengers, the extra tanks of helium 3, tools, and replacement parts for the damaged fusion reactor on board and then navigated the shuttle on a descending spiral toward the MTFP facility on the southeast rim of Bonestell Crater, a 43 km-wide 2,150 meter-deep circular impact crater. An oblong, semitransparent dome 25 meters high, two-hundred meters long, and 120-meters wide dominated the MTFP site. Connected to the main dome by a wide hundred meter long tube, a much smaller dome and several storage tanks sat at the edge of the crater. A large open-pit mine a few hundred meters north of the Bonestell Crater rim included two trucks that raised clouds of dust as they drove out of the pit toward the smaller dome. Some distance from the crater—named after Chesley Bonestell, the American artist who painted amazingly accurate pictures of Mars gleaned from the fuzzy telescopic images available in 1951—was now a deep lake filled with melt water that surrounded the central 3,651-meter peak. The shuttle flew over the nascent lake toward the southeast rim of the crater, where a large hangar next to the dome sat with its doors wide open. Chief engineer Hitachi maneuvered the shuttle inside the hangar and landed. They waited for a few minutes after the large doors closed and after a green light signaled normal pressure, they disembarked. Dr. Lindgren and her team were waiting at the bottom of the shuttle stairs to greet them.

Sera gave Josh a welcoming big hug. "It's been way too long since we last met," she said with a smile, "We don't have the pleasure of many visitors here on Mars."

Then after expressing her gratitude to Dr. Hitachi for bringing the Tesla team to Mars, she shook hands with the rest of the team and offered a special thank-you to the three reactor technicians. She then introduced Dr. Tsung-Dao Yang, the leading project scientist, Dr. Terry Bloomberg, the project geologist, and four other MTFP department heads.

"Now let me take you on a short tour of the main campus that we call UTD or 'Under the Dome.'"

A short access tube and an air lock connected the hangar to the UTD. The inner air lock door opened to a platform placed 7 meters above the UTD campus spread underneath the dome. As soon as Jerry stepped onto the platform, the pleasant warmth and fragrant humidity of the air reminded him of stepping off an airplane upon arrival in Hawaii. The light blue domed sky, indistinguishable from the big sky Jerry remembered from his days on a Montana ranch, radiated warmth from somewhere above, as white fluffy clouds drift across it. The campus under the dome encompassed 14 acres complete with flowering trees, plants, and a grass-filled park. Jerry counted fourteen small buildings surrounding one large central three-story building. Climbing down the platform steps, Sera led them on a tour of the campus that included the living quarters, recreational hall, auditorium, mess hall, kitchen, workrooms, and labs.

Sera pointed to the small windowless building and storage tanks at the far end of the campus. "The Bonestell station has two fusion reactors. "This fusion reactor provides all the necessary power needed for UTD, and the main fusion reactor outside the dome supplies power for the extraction plant. Nevertheless, we have a limited supply of helium 3 for the UTD reactor and lost all the helium 3 for the main reactor." Then after a pause she added, "Had we solely depended on the main reactor for all our UTD power and it went offline as it now has done, without power we would have to abandon this project and return to Earth within a few days. Your willingness to help us has made that eventuality unnecessary."

She led them into the large central building that contained the hydroponics gardens where healthy plants grew on two dozen long racks.

"We produce all our own food in this building for the seventy-eight folks housed at this station. Inside the hydroponics room and in the 'jungle,' we can grow everything from fruits to nuts and vegetables," Sera proudly announced.

She led them inside the high ceiling building designated as the "jungle" by a large sign over the airlock door. The temperature and humidity inside was noticeably higher than the rest of the UTD. Throughout the jungle, ferns, bushes, plants, and trees grew in profusion. Fragrant flowers and berries dressed the bushes and fruit trees, including oranges, papayas, bananas, and breadfruit. Butterflies big and small flittered about the bushes and trees. A large plot of red soil placed in a central clearing contained leafy plants growing in long neat rows. "Our vegetable garden," Sera said. Inside the hydroponics building, row after row of vegetables and fruits grew in large water-fed racks.

As they exited the jungle, Sera loaded everyone on three trams that then disappeared into the tube leading to the second smaller dome a hundred meters mile away from the UTD. Sera called the second dome "the factory," where three water and gas extraction buildings sat next to a central fusion reactor.

Terry Bloomberg took over from Sera to conduct the tour of the extraction factory.

"We process the Mars permafrost and regolith in the three extraction buildings fed by those trucks you saw excavating soil and ice from our open-pit mine just west of the Bonestell Crater." She pointed to three large pipes that entered and exited the large green building closest to the crater rim and then disappeared into the lake far below. "That is building 3, our water extraction factory. We send melted permafrost to the lake through those pipes," she explained. "The large blue pipe extending from the roof of building 2, our gasification factory, exits through the top of the factory dome where it returns CO_2 and nitrogen to the atmosphere."

"We brought 2 liters of helium 3 in canisters with us," Jerry said, pointing to two small tanks, "but this is only enough to last a few months. With your supply of helium 3 limited to the small storage tank in the UTD, will this be enough?"

Chief Scientist Yang smiled an inscrutable Chinese smile as he answered. "We extract helium 3 and metals from the Martian soil, melt water from the ice, and release nitrogen and carbon dioxide into the atmosphere. One of the differences on Mars is that it has an abundance of helium 3, which is rare on Earth but plentiful here, and the water contains twice as much dissolved metals per liter as that found in oceans on Earth. I think if you can help us get our fusion reactor back online and repair the damage to the gasification factory, we can become self-sufficient in a couple of months. The helium 3 you have brought along should suffice until then. What we need the most since the death of our technicians is your reactor technician's assistance. Tomorrow you can have a good look at the damage to the fusion reactor and building 3 and then evaluate what will be needed to restart the reactor and fix the gasification factory."

That evening Sera invited the Tesla folks to an open forum in the packed auditorium. As expected, the discussion centered on the Dorian gift and the fossil found on Sedna. A few scientists in the audience disputed that the artifact was a fossil, and others disputed the theory that Sedna had once orbited Nemesis. Many folks expressed disappointment that the Tesla folks hadn't brought the cube with them. Jerry showed a holograph of the cube and explained that his orders were to leave it safely stored on Tesla. He entertained conjecture about what the Dorian gift could possibly be. Some thought it would solve some mysteries in physics, cosmology, or astronomy. Others were certain that it would provide the technology needed for humans to visit the stars. Still others thought it would provide cures for diseases, genetic problems, and increase human longevity. Everyone had an opinion.

Dr. Vincent explained, "While we have been unable to get to the sphere inside the cube, the UWSF assures us that their labs will be able to do so. That is why we must return home as soon as possible after we help you repair your extraction factory."

Terry provided a history of the Terraforming Project for the Tesla visitors.

"I have been here at Bonestell for over twenty years working on Phase 1 of the Mars Terraforming Project, yet the first feasibility study at Bonestell began over fifty-five years ago, late in the twenty-first century soon after the first humans set foot on Mars. It was obvious that if humans were to colonize this planet, we couldn't do so by living under domes and dressed in space suits whenever outside. Unprotected, the inhospitable atmosphere of Mars would kill a human in minutes. At the time the first expedition set foot on this planet, the atmosphere consisted of carbon dioxide and nitrogen at a pressure less than that experienced on the summit of Mt. Everest. Although there were trillions of gallons of frozen water locked up in the aquifer, little of it made its way to the surface, and the small amount that did quickly evaporated. The thin dry atmosphere and lack of a global magnetic shield also provided little protection for living cells from ionizing radiation. Anyone venturing outside the UDT must wear a protective space suit and carry along a supply of oxygen. If humans are ever to colonize this planet, they must terraform the planet; thus, in the last century the UWSF managers funded the Mars Terraforming Project and built the original MTFP factory fifty-five years ago at Bonestell Creator.

Terry paused for questions and then continued when no one raised a hand.

"In the years since the UWSF built the UTD and extraction factory on Bonestell, the fusion reactor has heated enough permafrost to cover the entire Bonestell Crater floor with a lake over 140 meters deep. The project's factories have processed enough soil to release tons of CO_2 and nitrogen into the atmosphere. Those gasses have raised the Martian air pressure at the surface to 18 percent of that on Earth's surface. Mars is a cold planet, but due to the increased greenhouse CO_2 gas we have released, the average global temperature increased from -30 degrees C to -5 degrees C and remains above freezing during the Mars summer in some parts of the planet. Melting subsurface water is beginning to flow into some craters and soon we will introduce blue-green algae into those lakes. We have proven the terraforming idea and now we intended to advance to Phase-2 of the project and construct a dozen more extraction plants around Mars, which will release copious amounts of CO_2 and nitrogen into the thin Martian atmosphere and raise the surface temperature and pressure to sustainable levels. Large lakes will soon fill craters and depressions all over the Martian surface and by introducing oxygen-producing algae into those lakes, in a few hundred years Mars can have a breathable atmosphere."

"That is a long time before humans can walk on the surface without space suits," Gina commented.

"Yes, that is a long time to wait, but on Earth the oxygenation process took millions of years to produce a breathable atmosphere. Relatively speaking, two or three hundred years is not so very long," Terry said.

Sera thanked Terry for her presentation and closed the session. "Tomorrow we can begin to evaluate what must be done to bring the fusion reactor and the gasification factory back on line."

Early the following day the Tesla technicians inspected the extraction factory. They connected their canisters of helium 3 to the fusion reactor and after several hours were able to bring that reactor back online. However, the damage to the helium 3 and gasification factory was more extensive than expected. The accident not only breached the helium 3 storage tanks, but also damaged the helium 3 extraction equipment in the gasification factory. The technicians estimated that it would take three to four weeks to make repairs and bring the gasification factory back online. This news meant that since their shuttle could only make one round trip, Dr. Hitachi, Dr. Vincent, Jerry, Bill, Gina, and Dr. Mitera would be stuck on Mars for a month with little to do. Sera tried to soften their disappointment with the promise of a tour of Mars. She took them into the main auditorium and projected a large 3D topological map of Mars on a holographic screen. She then used a pointer to mark various locations on the map.

"The Bonestell Crater is located on Acidalia Planitia, a low-lying plane situated in north-central Mars. The plain is named after a matching albedo feature on a map by Giovanni Schiaparelli, who named the plain after the mythological fountain of Acidalia." She then moved the pointer some distance away from Bonestell and continued.

"We are building another factory on the Chryse Planitia or 'Golden Plain' southwest of Bonestell near the Viking Lander site. I thought you folks might like to take a tour of Mars and visit the original Viking 1

Lander site and the nearby Viking MTBF factory and then travel further south to see Copartes Chasma, which is the eastern part of the Valles Marineses or Mariner Valley better known as the Mars Grand Canyon. It will be a twelve-day 3,200-mile journey but the view is spectacular and a sight that anyone privileged enough to visit Mars must not miss. I have been there several times myself and am overwhelmed by the view on each visit."

Dr. Vincent thought that was an excellent idea, and everyone on his away team agreed.

"All right then, tomorrow morning at 0:700 Martian time we will meet on the entry platform to begin our tour," Sera said. "Remember to reset your chronometers for the 28-hour Martin Standard Time clock."

After everyone assembled on the platform, Sera led the team into the hangar where they parked the Tesla shuttle. Next to their shuttle were three Mars rovers, each similar to those the geological team used to explore Sedna. They prepared two of them for this journey. Sera split the away team into two groups; the first she assigned to travel with her on the rover named Austin, driven by MTFP engineer Paul Lindquist. Passengers Dr. Vincent, Jerry, and Gina joined three Bonestell technicians also assigned to Austin. Sera then named Dr. Hitachi, Bill Summerset, and Dr. Mitera with three other MTFP technicians and a mechanic to the second rover named Houston, led by Dr. Bloomberg and driven by MTFP engineer Shirley Tudor. The rovers waited as the hangar was depressurized and the large doors slowly opened. They drove out onto the Bonestell Crater rim, which rose over 100 meters from the surrounding Acidalia Planitia.

As the morning twilight sky brightened, Jerry watched as the weak orange-red sun rose over the horizon and painted the entire Martian sky from horizon to horizon a distinctive pink color. The Mars sky reminded him of a sunrise in the Montana Sky that predicted a storm, only pink rather than red. When above the horizon, the Martian sun seemed smaller and less brilliant than the sun to which he was accustomed. It not only colored the sky pink but also painted everything on the ground a monotonously dull rust color. Jerry looked out across the 4,500-foot deep Bonestell Crater toward the northern rim twenty-six miles away. Several thousand feet below the rim was Bonestell Lake that now filled the bottom of the crater. The lake appeared neither blue nor pink, but viewed against the red crater cliffs looked black. The most striking feature was the central island, its sharp peak rising 900 meters above the surface of the lake. To the south, the Acidalia lowlands region presented a mostly flat lowland plain that reminded Jerry of the Texas panhandle, except covered by rocks both big and small and not a speck of sagebrush or other greenery. Small jagged outcroppings and lone sentinels shaped by eons of relentless Martian wind marked the Planitia desert, otherwise covered by rust-colored sand that gathered in small undulating dunes. The few scattered craters reminded Jerry that he was not on Earth. The lowlands looked uninteresting and promised a monotonous drive across it.

"At least the Texas plains have a few plants and a farm here and there, but this Planitia desert is desolate," he said to Bill. Terry pointed toward the northeastern horizon and a low ridge that she called the Acidalia Mensa Mountains. To Jerry they looked like a few small weatherworn hills not worthy of calling "mountains." After a short pause, the rovers drove down the winding rim access road and out onto Acidalia Planitia. Fist-size rocks covered the desert floor and hundreds of large boulders, some the size of a truck, forced the rovers to pick a path between them. As they zigzagged their way through the boulder field, Sera explained their route.

"We will head southwest across the Acidalia and Chryse Planitia to the Viking MTFP factory that we are building near the first Viking Lander site almost 650 miles away," she explained. "Our Viking site is the second of twelve other planned MTFP factories that we will build over the next five years. Right now the only other human habitations on Mars besides our two MTFP factories is at New Bern, the 344-person scientific settlement located on the Amazonis Planitia east of the volcano Olympus Mons. Our rovers have a peak speed of 60 mph, but for safety's sake, we will only average about 40 mph. Therefore, the 1,200-mile trip to the Viking MTFP will take two long days. We should arrive at the Viking factory tomorrow just before sunset."

As they drove southwest across the Acidalia Planitia, the desolate and featureless lowlands fulfilled Jerry's prediction of a long, boring ride, so he decided to watch a video about Mars geology as they bounced along. The desert presented nothing interesting except for an occasional dust devil, swirling vortices of sand and dust that reached high into the sky. The Martian dust devils, similar to dust devils found in Texas, were far larger, more dangerous, and longer lived than those back on Earth. From the top of one high dune, Jerry counted no fewer than six devils swirling across the desert below. As they skirted one stadium-size crater, Sera noted that two of these whirling devils were moving right toward them. She told Paul to stop Austin and warned Shirley in Huston of the approaching devils. Both rovers prepared for the onslaught by closing all exhaust ports and engaging the window shutters. Jerry thought this was an unnecessary precaution until the first devil enveloped Austin. The intensity of the wind in the extremely thin atmosphere surprised him. It sounded like a freight train had engulfed Austin and the rover shook and swayed in the wind. The first devil passed over them in a few seconds and a minute later the second devil arrived. Sand was still falling from the sky from the first devil and a remnant cloud of dust hung in the air, making visibility impossible as the second devil struck. They waited for almost an hour while the dust and sand from both devils slowly settled back onto the ground before they could open the shutters. Because so much dust still floated in the air, the limited visibility forced them to rely on radar to pick their way across the desert and forced them to do so at a crawl.

"It would be reckless to drive across Acidalia at full speed and possibly end at the bottom of one of these craters," Sera said. "While driving across the Chryse Planitia, we lost one rover that drove into a crater and, because of the soft sand, couldn't climb out. This is a mistake that I don't wish to repeat."

About 3:00 PM and 320 miles from Bonestell, they came to the edge of a large ringed depression found at the edge of the gently rising Chryse Planitia, half of the way to the Viking factory.

"We have named this the Carlsbad Depression," Sera explained. "We think it is an old impact crater over 60 miles wide, 340 feet deep, and filled almost to the brim with loose sand. Because we have yet to decide if it would be safe to cross over it, we will stop here and wait until morning before we detour east around Carlsbad."

The next day they traveled across the rise of the Chryse Planitia and as the sun disappeared over the horizon, perched at the edge of a mile-wide crater, the Viking factory finally came into view. The Viking dome was about half the size of the one over the UTD at Bonestell. Next to the Viking dome was the same design of a three-building gasification factory and fusion reactor.

The drivers parked both rovers inside the hangar, and Sera and Shirley led the tourists and technicians into the Viking factory through an air lock. Not only was the Viking factory smaller than Bonestell, but it was also more utilitarian, lacking the amenities of the original. One building housed the living quarters and cafeteria, and Sera described the other six buildings as the fusion reactor, hydroponics building, and laboratories.

"This facility is still under construction, but we intend to have it online by next month," Shirley explained. "We will stay here overnight and tomorrow head out to visit the Viking Lander site, about 12 miles southeast from here, and then off across Chryse Planitia, Xanthe Terra, and Ophir Planum to Copartes Chasma, another 900 miles and a two-day journey away."

Early the next morning they loaded Austin and Huston with their passengers and drove the 12 miles to the Viking 1 Lander site. Everyone dressed in their space suits and walked over to where the Lander sat undisturbed for the past 143 years. The Lander was smaller than Jerry imagined, only four feet long and positioned on four spindly legs. Viking 1 glistened in the sunlight and looked pristine, except for the thin layer of red dust that covered the top surfaces of the craft.

"Viking 1 was the first American probe to land on Mars," Shirley said. "It wandered about the surface for six years, sending important pictures and soil sampling data back to Earth. The main mission was to test for living organisms, but it found no such signs of life."

"There is much controversy about that finding," Bill added. "One of the four onboard instruments found evidence of methane in the sample, a sign of living organisms. However, the other three experiments that heated the samples did not find any organics, so NASA declared the mission had failed to find signs of life. This decision caused scientists to argue for years. There are salts in the Martian soil that when heated by the three experiments probably destroyed any evidence of organic compounds. What Viking did find was plenty of silicon and iron, with significant amounts of magnesium, aluminum, sulfur, calcium, titanium, and trace elements, strontium and yttrium, in the soil."

"Later probes confirmed the findings of the methane instrument," Sera said. "Billions of years ago Mars had lots of surface water and simple one-celled organisms evolved. Yet Mars lost its surface water and today those organisms thrive beneath the permafrost. As our terraforming project warms the planet and fills the craters with water, these organisms will again bloom in the newly formed lakes. This can be a problem for our terraforming project. Even now, they are turning the water in Bonestell Lake a murky brown, and these native organisms will interfere with our efforts to introduce oxygen-producing algae. The oxygen so produced will eventually kill off the Martians because for them that gas is a deadly poison. Some folks argue that this is an ethical problem, and still others argue that we cannot be sure these organisms are native to Mars. Because the DNA of the Martian microbes is similar to those on Earth, there is a possibility that some of these organisms were transported from Earth to Mars and then evolved here."

The team went back to the rovers and settled down for the long trip across the Xanthe Terra. The terrain gradually increased from 1,200 feet below average global elevation to a few hundred feet above average elevation. Mottled with craters both large and small, Xanthe forced them to follow a zigzag southwest path as they crossed the plain. The rovers followed an ancient riverbed called Shulbatana Vallis until they came to a 31-mile-wide crater named Orson Welles, where they stopped for the evening. The next day they skirted the Orson crater and drove up onto the Ophir Planum, which rose to a height of 1,300 feet.

As they drove along, Terry took this opportunity to be a good tour guide.

"Valles Marineris, or Mariner Valley, is a vast canyon formation that runs along the Martian equator just east of the Tharsis region. Many side canyons dot the sides of the main canyon and extend for miles into the plains that surround the valley. The Marineris valley is 2500 miles long and reaches depths of up to four miles. For comparison, the Grand Canyon in Arizona is about 500 miles long and one mile deep. The canyon extends from the Noctis Labyrinthus region in the west to the chaotic terrain in the east, or about one-fifth of the planet's entire girth. Most researchers agree the valley is a large tectonic crack in the Martian crust that formed as the planet cooled and forced the surface to split apart. Erosion enlarged the crack to its present width and depth and created the largest canyon in the solar system. The Copartes valley displays layered deposits more defined there than in the rest of the canyon. These deposits predate the Valles Marineris canyon, suggesting erosion and sedentary processes are mostly responsible for the later formation of the valley."

That afternoon the rovers parked about 25 yards away from the edge of the canyon and, after everyone donned space suits, they walked over to the edge of the canyon, where the Ophir plain simply seemed to fall away into an abyss. Jerry had visited the Grand Canyon several times before but it couldn't compare with the majesty of this canyon. He peered over the edge of the cliff to view the floor that lay 26,000 feet or 4 miles below them and suddenly felt a surge of vertigo. He took a couple of steps back from the edge and waited for his dizziness to subside. When his head cleared, from a safer distance he tried to spot the other side of the canyon 60 miles away, but it was barely visible in the prevailing haze. He cautiously stepped closer to the edge so he could view the canyon floor without experiencing another bout of vertigo. Except for the alluvial fans that spread beneath the bottom of the cliffs, the valley floor was flat and featureless, although he could see a hint of an extinct river channel. Every part of the canyon took on a rusty hue, with little variation in that monotonous color. The viewpoint looked over Horseshoe Bowl, a natural notch in the cliff that formed a half-circle around them and provided a clear view the cliff itself. The layers of compacted soil and gravel that overlaid each other testified to the sedimentary nature of the Copartes canyon. Deep furrows on the flanks of the cliffs reminded Jerry of the layered cliffs of the Grand Canyon and provided clear evidence that flowing water formed those channels.

"No doubt Mars was once a wet world," Terry claimed. "Two billion years ago, a large river fed by many surrounding tributaries flowed down the canyon floor to a vast inland sea and eroded this valley into what we see today. Given a few hundred years, our Terraforming Project will allow water to flow again into the Valles Marineris and the sea will grow."

They slept overnight in the rovers, and the following morning revisited the Horseshoe Bowl observation outlook to view the canyon when lit by the morning sun, which created deep shadows and outlined some of the features better than the setting sun had done.

Everyone except Sera and Jerry returned to the rovers. As they stood together at the edge of the cliff, Sera shared some of her thoughts about the cube.

Jerry, I find the circumstances surrounding the Dorian gift most odd," she began. "Why for instance have they made access to their gift so difficult for us?"

Jerry conceded that this also confused him, but he surmised they designed the cube to protect it over the eons of time it would have to wait for discovery. "It had to be robust enough to survive for all those millions of years."

Sera thought for a moment and then continued. "I'm sure you know the story about the Trojan horse, but let me remind you of the similarities between that historical tale and the cube. The Greek army had been unable to breach the walls of the Trojan city for over a year. Discouraged, the Greeks packed up, boarded their ships, and pretended to leave for home. They left a large wooden horse outside the gates of the city as a gift of atonement. The Trojans opened the gate and dragged the gifted horse into the city, and that night several soldiers who had remained hidden inside the horse climbed out and opened the gates, after which the Greeks stormed the city and declared victory."

Sera paused to let the analogy sink in.

"I think the Dorians have deliberately made access to the cube difficult so you would have to take it back to Earth to open it. I don't know what their gift may be, perhaps something wonderful, but I would be cautious when opening it. It could also be something very dangerous."

"A Trojan horse... an interesting thought," Jerry conceded. "We were unable to record the Dorian message projected in the chamber, but for me the Dorian representative was believable and honest with his story and his promise of a gift that would benefit humankind. I do not think it was a ruse."

"Perhaps not, but in my mind something is fishy about this so-called 'gift.' I know the scientists on the Lassell Station would have been thorough when they analyzed the cube. The Dorians encased their gift in a container so well designed that they obviously never intended for the finders to open it even with the most advanced technology available to them. They intended that the finders would return the cube to Earth.

You must convince the UWSF to exercise extreme caution when opening the cube."

"Sera, thank you for the warning. I will share your 'Trojan Horse' concern with Dr. Vincent and I am sure he will do so with the UWSF folks."

After everyone was back on the rovers, Sera prepared for the long journey home.

"We can skip revisiting the Viking MTFP site and instead visit the Pathfinder landing site on our way home," she said.

They drove northwest across Ophir Planum to the west of the 130 miles-wide Mutch and 110 miles-wide Nanedi Craters and out onto Chryse Planum to the Pathfinder Landing site. Pathfinder landed in Ares Valles in 1997 where the little rover Sojourner remained when its solar panel and batteries finally gave out. A protective wire fence enclosed the Pathfinder site and a rock monument with an embedded copper plaque explained the Pathfinder mission. Sojourner measured 24 inches long and 18 inches wide, with the top covered by a solar panel. It was clear why the extraordinarily successful mission had finally ended: a thick layer of red dust covered the solar panel, preventing it from recharging the batteries.

They remained overnight at the Pathfinder site, and the next day headed out for Bonestell, 930 miles distant. Their northward path followed Tiu Valles that emptied onto the featureless Acdalia Plantia. As they drove out onto Acdalia, they came to two large side-by-side craters, each over 100 miles in diameter. A narrow gap five miles wide separated the two craters.

"Rather than drive around these craters which would take hours, we will continue north driving in the gap between them," Sera said.

Two miles inside the gap, they came to a formation of narrow upright rocks of varying sizes and heights. The jagged monoliths sat side by side in an arc extending across the gap toward both bordering craters.

Sera consulted her map and then took some readings with her imaging scope. "These rocks are the rim of an ancient crater that does not show up on my map. It is a little less than 2 miles in diameter but has been filled to the brim with sand. While it is risky to drive across these sand-filled craters, retreating out of the gap and skirting those large craters will take another day, so we are going to drive straight across this little crater."

Paul cautioned Sera, reminding her of the rover they lost in just such a crater some years ago. "Some of these sand-filled craters contain sandpits, which look deceptively solid but are dangerous and hard to see. Water saturates some of these pits and creates a surface that is like quicksand."

Sera appreciated the danger and warned Shirley on Huston to keep a sharp lookout for any change in the surface that might indicate a sandpit.

"Because the sand underneath the surface of these pits is wet, they will look a little darker than the surrounding sand, but this is not always the case. Look for a slight depression sometimes only a foot or two deep."

Paul drove Austin into the crater and Shirley followed with Huston. Paul kept a sharp lookout for any change in the color of the sand or a slight depression, but the crater presented the same monotonous landscape as everywhere else on Mars. All seemed to be going well until Austin's left tracker lost traction.

"I think we are teetering on the edge of one of those damn sandpits," Paul said. He tried to back out, but then the other tractor began to slip in the soft sand. The more Paul tried to extricate Austin from the pit, the deeper it dug itself in.

Shirley was watching Paul struggle with Austin. "Paul, stop what you are doing. It will only make your situation worse. We will hook a cable up to Austin and try to pull you out of the pit."

One of the Huston mechanics, Joe Trent, dragged a cable over to Austin and hooked it onto the rover. Joe stood by at the edge of the pit and watched as Shirley tried to drag Austin out of the pit.

"STOP!" Joe shouted. "Austin is sinking further into the pit. My feet were sinking in the quicksand as I hooked the cable up to Austin. Everyone should get out of Austin right now before the pit swallows both Austin and its passengers."

Sera told everyone to dress in their space suits and get out of Austin as quickly as possible. Jerry was the first one out and as he exited Austin, he could see that the sand had fully engulfed the left tractor and half of the right tractor, causing the rover to lean at a 20-degree angle. Jerry had to keep his feet moving to prevent his boots from sinking in the soft sand.

"Sera, tell everyone that once they get out onto the sand, they have to keep moving toward Huston. Anyone who stands still will sink into the pit."

When everyone had safely arrived beside Joe at the edge of the pit, they stood there and watched as Austin slowly sank deeper and deeper into the pit until only the roof and antennas were visible.

"Now we have a problem," Sera said. "While it may be uncomfortable, we can fit everyone inside Huston. Nevertheless, the rover is not equipped to accommodate seventeen people for four full days of travel to backtrack and then skirt those large craters and travel back to Bonestell. The rover just doesn't have the water, oxygen, and food to sustain this many passengers for the entire trip."

"We still need to get through the gap, but if we are careful and send someone to walk in front of the rover we can avoid the sandpits. The gap is only another five miles long, but after we emerge we will still be 600 miles away from Bonestell, a full two day's travel," Dr. Bloomberg said.

"So what do you suggest?" Paul asked.

"I will contact the folks at Bonestell MTFP and ask them to bring another shuttle to meet us and transport part of the team back to Bonestell," Sera said.

Sera contacted the folks at Bonestell and they agreed to meet Huston at the Richardson Crater, about half of the way back and a day's travel for each. They met the shuttle at a point 300 miles from Bonestell Crater, transferred the Austin team, and then together made the trip back to the MTFP facility.

After arriving back at UTD, the away team met with Dr. Tsung-Dao Yang and the three Tesla reactor technicians for an update. Dr. Yang reported that the helium 3 extraction factory and gasification operation was back online.

"Then the Tesla team will prepare to return to our ship," Dr. Vincent said.

The following day Captain Ferguson and his Tesla away team said good-bye to the Bonestell folks and boarded their shuttle for the return trip to Tesla. Tesla had remained parked in orbit while Dr. Vincent and his away team visited Mars. Everyone celebrated the away team's return, for it meant they would now resume the last part of their journey, the trip from Mars to the moon and home.

Chapter Nine
Homecoming

June 5, 2125

Wasting no time, Dr. Ferguson immediately broke orbit around Mars and began the five-month journey toward a rendezvous with the moon. Jerry and Wendy made their way to the observation room as soon as they felt the gentle force produced as Tesla accelerated. They had enough argon remaining to achieve an eventual velocity of 123,000 mph in three weeks of constant acceleration, and then a little less than a month later they would rotate Tesla 180 degrees and begin breaking for insertion into moon orbit.

"We are on our way home … again," Jerry said as he watched Mars shrink. "But Sera shared something that has been bothering me."

Jerry told Wendy about Sera's Trojan Horse warning about the cube.

"I have to agree with Sera. She expressed a valid concern," Wendy said. "I have never understood why the Dorians made access to their gift so difficult."

"I shared her concern with Dr. Vincent," Jerry said, "but convinced the Dorians made the cube robust to protect the gift, he dismissed Sera's warning. He claimed the USWA lab in Nevada will have better technology than on Tesla or on the Lassell Station and I'm sure that they can safely open the cube."

Just before Tesla began to rotate three weeks later, the view from the observation room was splendid. Mercury and Venus shone close to the blocked-out image of the sun, while Earth and its moon were a hand's width away.

"Look, there is our planet—that *little blue marble* spaced some distance from the sun!" Wendy exclaimed as she adjusted the telescope to view Earth. She increased the magnification and let out a deep sigh.

"Jerry, come over here to the telescope and have a look. Earth is the most beautiful planet in the solar system!" Wendy exclaimed.

"Put it on the monitor," Jerry suggested. Wendy increased the magnification and the orb dressed in wispy clouds appeared. Despite the intervening clouds, both the North and South American continents were clearly visible. Wendy continued to increase the magnification until the West Coast of North America filled the screen.

"Look, you can even make out California and the San Francisco Bay area!" Wendy said as her excitement grew.

After an absence of several years, the view of home was so tantalizing close that it triggered a bittersweet realization for both Jerry and Wendy. In two short months, they would be home and return to their former lives. Their friendship had grown from mere colleagues and shipmates into a loving relationship that softened the isolation and loneliness in deep space. Wendy once admitted that without this bond, she could not have endured the long, lonely voyage. Jerry felt much the same way. Now it would soon end and as Shakespeare once wrote, "parting is such sweet sorrow."

****

November 10, 2125

Five months after breaking Mars orbit, Jerry and Wendy watched as the moon gradually filled the view screen and Tesla effortlessly inserted itself into an orbit around Earth's satellite. Two years late and over eight years since leaving moon orbit, the Tesla crew and passengers were now only a short shuttle journey from home and soon would be reunited with their friends and family. The long delayed voyage home had ended. That evening, Dr. Ferguson and the crew of Tesla held a farewell dinner for their passengers. They shared a few tears and many warm handshakes between those who had been travel partners for these years. Dr. Vincent gave a thank-you speech for the wonderful treatment he and his colleagues had received on Tesla. Dr. Ferguson announced that Tesla would now begin to prepare for another deep space journey, this time to carry the often-delayed expedition team to Pluto where they will establish a base and explore the surface of that neglected minor planet.

Jerry spent the next morning getting ready to board the shuttle back to the Lompoc Base in California. To avoid possible contamination, the UWSF instructed him to seal the cube and fossils in their own individual containers. He did so and placed the containers in his backpack. Then he packed a few personal items in an overnight bag and met Josh in the shuttle bay. They would not be going directly home from Lompoc because the UWSF director, Dr. Marvin Ingram, ordered Jerry and Dr. Vincent to fly direct from Lompoc to the UWSF Yucca Mountain test site labs northwest of Las Vegas and to bring the fossils and the cube with them.

As soon as the shuttle arrived at Lompoc, Jerry and Josh were ushered onto a flight that arrived that evening at the UWSF Yucca Mountain Science Laboratories (YMSL) located deep within Yucca Mountain in Nevada. A ground jitney was waiting for them at the Yucca Mountain airport. A wide cave marked the entrance to YMSL site where they boarded a maglev train that whisked them deep inside the mountain. Originally designed as a nuclear waste depository, the site had been redesigned as the main UWSF research laboratories. Because the area was prone to earthquakes, in the twentieth century the AEC abandoned the Yucca Mountain site. Discounting the earthquake danger, the UWSF converted the depository to a Level-One Science Research Laboratory designated SRL-L1 and equipped it with all the latest scientific instruments and equipment.

Dr. Ingram and his assistant met Josh and Jerry as they exited the maglev and, after a brief introduction, led them into the negative pressure clean room found deep inside the sprawling SRL-L1 analysis lab where they met the director of metrology, Dr. Abe Reston, the director of genetics, Dr. Mary Bartel, and the paleontology lab director, Dr. Susan Cartwright.

Dr. Cartwright asked Jerry for the Sedna fossils, which he gave to her except for the original fossil that he and Bill discovered. He felt ownership of that fossil which he kept in his backpack.

"We will perform a visual examination of the cube before subjecting it to instrument analysis and dissection," Dr. Reston announced.

Once inside and properly dressed in clean room attire, they entered the room and Dr. Reston told Jerry to place the container holding the cube on a marble laminar flow table housed inside a glass containment enclosure.

"Dr. Abrams, I assume the container hasn't been opened since it was sealed on Tesla?" Dr. Reston asked as Jerry laid the container on the table.

"Yes. It has remained intact since I sealed the cube container back on Tesla. Jerry stepped away as the enclosure lid closed with a hissing sound and air began to flow across the table. Two scientists fully dressed in clean room outfits reached through ports in the side of the glass enclosure, removed the cube from the containment box, and checked its temperature and radiation, which as always measured 104 degrees Fahrenheit with no measurable radiation.

Dr. Ingram and his team watched as the scientists turned on lights that bathed the cube in brilliant illumination. One scientist held the cube and rotated it so they could closely examine each side of the cube.

"I thought you said there were no visible markings on any side of the cube?" Dr. Ingram asked Jerry.

"There aren't," he answered, surprised at the question.

"Take a closer look at the cube," Dr. Ingram challenged. "You can see a hairline crack that extends across the entire face on one side of the cube."

Indeed a hairline crack extended diagonally from one edge of the cube to the other as Jerry looked at the exposed face.

"I assure you that this crack wasn't there two days ago when I placed the cube in its sealed storage box. And as I said, the box has not been opened since then."

They continued to examine each side of the cube and while they watched, a second crack suddenly appeared on another side, and then a third and a fourth until all faces displayed several hairline cracks.

"The cube is breaking apart as we watch," Dr. Ingram said.

"Why now?" Jerry said with amazement.

"The only test that we were not able to perform on the cube was to subject it to the gravity that it would experience when on Earth. I think that now that we are here on Earth, the cube is responding to Earth's gravity," Dr. Vincent suspected.

Over the next few minutes, more cracks appeared on each face and then each began to widen.

"See if it will now come apart," Dr. Weston suggested.

The scientist took a hold of opposite sides of the cube and gently pulled. It easily separated into two unequal parts, exposing the internal sphere which remained attached to the larger piece. He placed the two parts of the cube on the table. For a few minutes, each part continued to crumble until all that remained was a pile of gray sand that covered the 7 cm-diameter silver sphere. They carefully extracted the sphere from the pile and noticed that a thick green slime was slowly dripping onto the table from a pinhole in the sphere.

"This pile of sand won't tell us much," Dr. Reston lamented while ignoring green slime dripping from the sphere. "We may never be able to find out about the cube's metrology and why no one could penetrate it or how it kept its internal temperature of 104 degrees for 65 million years. Damn, there was so much to learn from this container."

Dr. Bartel ignored Dr. Rreston's rant and focused on the green slime that began to pool up on the table.

She told one of her assistants to take a sample of the green substance and place it under the microscope. He extracted a pea-size sample of green slime and placed it under a microscope so Dr. Bartel could examine it.

After exploring the sample for a couple of minutes, she looked up from the microscope and said, "The sample contains hundreds of nucleated cells, and each cell is alive and dividing."

Everyone including Jerry and Josh took a turn to look through the microscope.

Jerry did not try to hide is disillusionment and utter disgust.

"So, this is our so-called Dorian gift. It's just a bunch of damn cells and definitely not the so-called 'gift' the Dorian had promised us. We brought an alien seedpod back to Earth with us."

"Not just any cells, but alien cells," Dr. Vincent said, obviously trying to mitigate Jerry's disappointment.

"It all makes sense to me now," Jerry said. "The Dorians never intended for us to open the cube. The promise of a Dorian gift was a ruse to encourage us to take their seedpod back to Earth where gravity would cause it to open. Their story that the cube contained something wonderful, a gift for all humankind, was a clever lie intended to entice us to transport their seeds back to Earth. The cube is a Trojan Horse, the Dorian plan to repopulate their species millions of years after they abandoned Earth to find another more suitable planet to preserve their species. Because the Earth's surface is so dynamic, there was no safe place on Earth to leave the cube while the planet recovered from the asteroid tragedy. They left the cube on Sedna knowing that intelligent beings in the distant future would find it and bring it back to Earth. This is how they intended to introduce their spawn on Earth even if it took millions of years to do so. Eventually they intended to displace whatever sentient species had evolved on Earth with their own species. These aliens are untrustworthy, self-serving, and perverse. I especially resent their sanctimonious garbage about their prime directive, which would not allow them to affect our world's natural process of evolution. The only prime directive they have is to spread their species."

"That is a bit harsh, Jerry," Dr Vincent said. "Perhaps they intended to coexist on Earth with us, but thank God we did not try to open the cube until we were in this lab. If we had done so once we arrived back on Earth, the cube could have scattered the Dorian seeds into our environment. Nevertheless, Jerry may be right. We must destroy those cells before they have a chance to escape."

"Not to worry—none of these cells are ever going to escape from this facility," Dr. Ingram assured him.

"I agree with Dr. Vincent," Jerry argued. "These cells are a biohazard that can annihilate our species and represent the greatest danger that humanity has ever faced. They must be destroyed."

"No, that is not going to happen, not now … not ever," Dr. Ingram said with final resolve.

Dr. Bartel had a look of horror on her face. "You cannot be serious about wanting to destroy them. Scientists have a duty to explore the unknown. These cells are unique, the first evidence of alien life that humanity has discovered. We must nurture and grow them so we can study and understand about this alien life."

Jerry disagreed. "This was part of the Dorian plan B. They knew we would be curious and nurture their cells. What you may learn about aliens does not justify the risk these cells pose for humans. For all you know you might grow Dorian monsters dedicated to eradicating us from the planet. You don't fully understand what you are dealing with. We must destroy these cells … now."

Dr. Ingram dismissed their concerns. "It is impossible for the alien cells to escape this facility, and what we may learn about them will further our understanding of alien life."

"The Yucca Science lab is an airtight level-one facility buried deep in Yucca Mountain with no possible way for these cells or anything else to escape. It will be safe for us to grow and keep the alien cells right here so we can study them," Dr. Bartel added.

"Just like the Ebola experiment in Atlanta that was fully contained but somehow escaped level-1 confinement in 2034 and caused an epidemic that killed thousands of Americans?" Jerry reminded Dr. Bartel.

"No, that was a level-1 surface facility with inadequate security. A careless employee let the virus escape. Our security and employee vetting is thorough. Such a catastrophe can never happen here," she said with self-righteous conviction.

As they argued, a biologist from Dr. Bartel's lab who had continued examining the cells under the high-power microscope interrupted the discussion.

"The nucleus of these cells contains DNA," he reported, "and I have been able to analyze it. It is unusual DNA, but DNA nevertheless. These cells are alive. They contain 48 chromosomes and they can swiftly reproduce, and in fact they have already divided four times."

Dr. Bartel looked again through the microscope. "The individual cells are indeed dividing and differentiating into organized cells at an unprecedented rate," she commented.

Dr. Ingram turned his attention back to Jerry and Josh.

"You have witnessed what is perhaps the most important biological discovery of all times, a reproducing alien life-form. You must never tell anyone what you witnessed here today. I am ordering you to remain silent about everything you have seen."

Jerry used every ounce of self-control not to blow up at Dr. Ingram. He turned to Josh who remained stone-faced and said nothing in response to Dr. Ingram's admonition.

Jerry stammered, "Never talk about it? The world has the right to know the truth about the Dorians and their so-called gift. My lips will definitely **not** remain sealed," he almost shouted.

"They had better be sealed, or you will be fired from UC Berkeley and in addition you may be prosecuted for disclosing UWSF classified information. The Foundation will discredit you should you talk about alien cells. We will put out a press release tomorrow and claim that because of the millions of years the cube sat on Sedna, the Dorian gift had deteriorated to the point where we couldn't recover anything of value from inside the cube. If you say otherwise, we will accuse you of lying and making up a story to gain personal publicity. You are strictly charged not to speak with anyone about alien cells … not now, not ever."

"Why do you want to hide this discovery from the world," Jerry asked. "Doesn't everyone have the right to know the truth about these dishonest and self-serving Dorians and that we have alien cells that are reproducing?"

"The world isn't ready for this revelation. Folks would panic and insist that we destroy the alien cells, just as you are arguing to do right now."

Jerry was about to continue his argument when Dr. Ingram said, "Enough talk."

He then called for two security guards to escort Jerry and Josh out of the Yucca Mountain Science labs and see to it that they return by air to Burbank. "Keep my warning in mind," he said as they departed.

On the flight to Burbank, Josh suggested that they take Dr. Ingram's threat seriously. "Jerry, let's think this over before we talk to anyone. If we say anything about the Dorian cells, Dr. Ingram will follow through with his threats and, in the end, the UWSF will discredit both of us. Our careers will be in ruin and we will become pariahs in the scientific world."

"For now I will keep my mouth shut," Jerry promised, "but only until I have some time to ponder it. For now all I want to think about is seeing Carol and Aden again."

As soon as Jerry and Josh deplaned in Burbank, a horde of eager reporters met them with notepads ready and then shoved microphones in their faces.

"Could the UWSF scientists open the cube? What was the Dorian gift inside?"

Josh looked at Jerry and then pushed through the reporters as he said, "We have no comment right now. The UWSF managers will give you a press release tomorrow. It is best that you wait for their official press release."

"The world has been waiting for yeas to learn about the Dorian gift. Why won't you share something about it?"

"We prefer that you hear the details from the UWSF folks," Josh said curtly as he caught the subway to Caltech.

Jerry called Carol from the airport and then caught the next maglev train from Burbank to Fremont. Carol and Aden were waiting for him on the platform. As he and Carol embraced for the first time in over eight years, her hug dispelled the concern that his reception would be cool at best. Carol's arms wrapped about him in a genuine, warm, and long embrace followed by a kiss. He knew that Carol must be aware of his affair with Wendy, but if she felt any resentment or anger, she didn't show it. Aden stood a few steps behind Carol and Jerry as they embraced. After the kiss, Jerry moved toward his son who he now barely recognized. The last time he saw him he was a boy and now he was a fully-grown young man twenty years old and would soon graduate from Stanford University with an MS in physics. Both men felt a bit awkward, so they didn't embrace but shook hands, which was warm and genuine. On the way home, Aden wanted to hear all about the Dorian cube and the gift inside. Jerry explained that they had opened the cube but he couldn't disclose any information about the cube "opening" or the gift inside. Everyone would have to wait for tomorrow and the announcements from the UWSF information manager.

"That is strange, Dad. You were there when they opened the cube, so why can't you talk about what was inside?"

"I was there, but I have been strictly forbidden to talk about it."

Aden leaned forward from the backseat. "The world has been waiting for years to hear about this so-called gift. It makes no sense the UWSA will not allow you to tell everyone what you know about the gift."

"Perhaps the director just wants to be the first one with the news," Jerry offered.

The rest of the way home the talk was about Stanford, Jerry's mom and dad, and Jerry's travel to Sedna and his travels on Triton and Mars. No one asked again about the "gift."

Homecoming was everything that Jerry anticipated. When they arrived at their San Francisco home, a crowd of friends, neighbors, and relatives including Jerry's mom and dad were waiting outside to greet him. The moment he stepped out of the car, everyone crowed around him. Folks peppered him with questions and most of all they wanted to know about the Dorian gift. Jerry hugged his mom and dad and fended off the barrage of questions. He promised to say more tomorrow, after the UWSF announcement and when he had a chance to rest. He then excused himself and with his family went inside his house. A few minutes later, the local TV and newspaper media showed up at the front door.

Jerry asked Aden to tell the reporters that he was not giving interviews. The reporters were nothing if not persistent. Aden had to force the front door closed and ignored the doorbell and knocking. Jerry's satellite phone and front door bell continued to ring for the next several hours.

The UWSF press release from Dr. Ingram the next day satisfied almost no one. He claimed that over millions of years, the gift had deteriorated and the information inside the sphere was lost forever. The press release especially angered Dr. Vincent's Sedna team who were witnesses to the Dorian message and knew the Dorians had gone to too much trouble to ensure that their gift would remain intact for it to have simply deteriorated. They all knew that this was a ruse intended to distract the public from whatever gift was inside. The calls on Jerry's satellite phone increased, but he did not answer any of them, even those from his team members.

Yet Jerry needed to talk to someone about his experience at Yucca Mountain, and who was better to confide in than Carol. After urging her to keep his confidence, Jerry shared the truth about the Dorian gift.

Carol didn't immediately react to Jerry's story. She took a minute to ponder, and then looking deep into Jerry's eyes, smiled. "The experiment the UWSF managers are conducting in their lab is a threat for all humanity. They don't have the right to conceal that they are growing alien cells in their lab. Everyone needs to know that the UWSF is unilaterally performing their own little experiment to learn more about these aliens. Jerry, you and Josh need to tell the world about the danger this experiment poses. Should these cells escape, it could spell the end of humanity."

"You're absolutely right, but the USWA folks will discredit us and contradict anything we say about what we saw in Yucca Mountain. They control the university system and although I am a tenured professor at UC Berkeley, they will pressure the chancellor to fire me from my position. For now, Josh and I have agreed to remain silent, but this forced silence is eating away at me."

Two days later Jerry received a delayed video from Dr. Sera Lindgren at the MTFP on Mars.

"Jerry, I heard the UWSF folks were able to open the cube but found nothing usable inside. I don't believe that story for one minute. As I suggested, I think the cube may have been a Trojan Horse, a seedpod intended to spread their genetic material on Earth. I'm convinced that this is what the UWSF scientists discovered inside the cube and they are now hiding that fact. You and Josh were there when they opened the cube and you have a moral duty to tell the world what you witnessed. If it was as I suspect a Dorian seedpod, then you must disclose what you saw."

Sera's assumption was right on, and others, especially other members of the Sedna geological team who were inside the Dorian chamber with Josh and Jerry, sent e-mails encouraging him to speak out.

Peter Ramos spoke plainly about Dr. Ingram's press conference in his voice mail to Jerry. "He is lying through his rotten teeth," he said. "We know that the cube had kept the gift well protected for millions of years, and now the UWSF folks are keeping the secret to themselves, and for whatever reason I cannot even imagine."

Jerry began to wonder if the UWSF people could keep the truth under wraps. Someone at UWSF is bound to talk about the alien seeds.

Six weeks after returning to San Francisco, Jerry reluctantly made the journey across the bay to his office at UC Berkeley. His first office visitor was the geology department director who welcomed him back and asked if he would give a lecture about his Sedna experiences. Obviously, no one had warned the director that Jerry might say something unauthorized. Jerry agreed to do so the following week. The second visitor to his office was Wendy. Her greeting was strained and guarded, and she seemed agitated.

"Jerry, I listened to the press release from Dr. Ingram and his information officer about the Dorian gift. You and I both know that press release was total bullshit. I don't buy the UWSF story that the gift had deteriorated over the ages while it waited for discovery. The Dorians knew it would be millions of years before intelligent beings would evolve and discover their gift, so they encased it in a robust container. Yet it wasn't necessary to design the container to be impenetrable. They had another motive in doing this. You were at the Yucca Mountain lab when they opened the cube and now you and Josh know what was inside. You must both tell the world about the Dorian gift."

"I'm sorry Wendy, but Josh and I have been strictly forbidden to talk about what was inside the cube. For now, I am keeping my mouth shut."

Wendy frowned. "Obviously there is something weird and wonderful about the gift, something the UWSF managers do not want the world to know. You and Josh saw what was inside. You must not let those bureaucrats intimidate you and remain silent. The truth about the Dorian gift is too important for a few UWSF scientists to keep the truth from the world. I think Sera had it right with her Trojan Horse theory. I don't care what they have threatened you with, you must speak out."

After Wendy left, Jerry called Josh and told him about his scheduled lecture.

"The title of my lecture next Wednesday at 7:00 PM in the Jewett Auditorium will be "Sedna and the Dorians" and in this talk I am going to expose the Dorian ruse and their eventual plan to inherit the Earth. I am also going to describe what I witnessed as the Yucca Mountain scientists opened the cube. I would like you to be there with me."

After a pause, Josh responded. "Last week Dr. Ingram invited me to revisit the lab at Yucca Mountain, and I was able to see how far the Dorian experiment had progressed in only a few weeks. Jerry, it was like that old twentieth century movie, *The Pod People*. A half-dozen glass incubators each filled with nutrient fluid supported a developing embryo, but not like any embryo that I ever saw. The best description I can make is that they looked like an alligator embryo, about the size of a football. They had dissected one embryo and preserved its internal organs in glass jars. You could make out certain organs, like a heart and lungs, and a large brain, but the other organs were as none other found in earth mammals. Dr. Ingram showed me a composite picture of what this creature might look like when fully grown. It looked nothing like the Dorian we saw in the Sedna chamber. That holographic projection was not Dorian, but a humanoid fabrication intended to gain our confidence. The composite picture depicted a bipedal creature more reptilian than human. The picture turned my stomach and I had to look away. Yet what frightened me even more is the UWSF folks are convinced that they have full control of their experiment. I'm not so sure they do. Even worse is that they are clueless about what to do with the alien embryos once they are *born*. Will they destroy sentient beings or allow them to fully mature? And once fully grown, how do they intend to keep the aliens in check?"

Jerry paused before he responded. "So, doesn't this make you even more convinced that we must both tell our story and lobby to stop this dangerous research? Dr. Ingram is naively cooperating with the Dorian plan B."

"If we decide to go public with what we know, it will be an uphill battle to get our story out and have folks consider it credible," Josh argued. "UWSF is powerful and has control of the media. In the end, they will discredit us and the media will depict you and me as dissident malcontents. We will become scientists without jobs."

"Well, I have to do what I have to do. I can survive without UC Berkeley. I wish I could convince you to join me next Wednesday."

"I'll think about it," Josh finally said. "Save me a seat."

When the evening arrived for Jerry's lecture, folks packed the Jewett Auditorium to overflowing and the media folks stood in the back ready to record his every word.

At 7:00 PM, Jerry strode to the podium, surveyed his audience, and noticed the empty seat in the front row that he had reserved for Josh. He began his lecture by describing their first and second expeditions on Sedna. He told about their discovery of the cave and that they had accessed the Dorian archives. Then he detailed how they opened the door and about the Dorian holographic video and the promise of a wonderful gift inside the cube. Finally, he told about the fossil he discovered, which now was in the hands of the UC Berkeley Paleontology Department. Yet the crux of his lecture followed.

"Our astronomers have surmised the Dorian home belonged to a system in the Orion Constellation about twelve light-years from our sun. More than sixty-four million years ago, their sun, now a white dwarf, had run out of hydrogen and was expanding into its red giant phase. Soon their planet would become uninhabitable. The prime directive of the Dorian civilization was to ensure that they could continue their species, and to do so they drew up a migration plan. They had discovered hundreds of potentially habitable worlds circling other star systems and one included our own Earth. To continue their species, they sent hundreds of starships into space each with a different destination. They trusted that at least a few Dorians would eventually reach habitable worlds that would allow them to sustain their species. The laws of physics and the tremendous distances between stars dictated that their journey would be long, requiring centuries of travel. Only their great grandchildren would ever see their designated destination. Yet it was their only hope for survival as a species and they are a very patient people. Sixty-five million years ago, a Dorian spaceship finally arrived on Earth, but it arrived when our planet's environment had been decimated by the Chicxulub asteroid impact in Mexico. This disaster destroyed most of the plants and animals on Earth and made the planet an inhospitable place for their race to prosper. They would eventually become as extinct as all the large animals who were trying to scratch out a living on this desolate planet that would take thousands of years to recover. Conditions forced them to move on."

Jerry showed a slide rendition of the Chicxulub event.

"Their mission to settle on Earth had failed, yet they devised a plan B. If they couldn't wait for the time it would take for Earth to recover from the asteroid impact, then perhaps they could leave their spawn in the form of preserved seeds that could be resurrected when the Earth would be more hospitable for their species. Because Earth's geology is so dynamic, it was not a safe place to leave their seedpod there. Instead, they left a seedpod on a remote planet, trusting that someday an intelligent space-faring species would find it and return it to Earth. Protected by the cube and containing their cells and DNA, the pod should remain viable for millions of years. They left a message and the promise of a wonderful gift for those who discovered the archive, a gift well protected by the impenetrable cube."

Jerry showed a holographic image of the cube on the large screen.

"Their holographic message portrayed the Dorians as a benevolent race only searching for a new home. The Dorian claimed that because their prime directive forbade interference with the natural evolution of an emerging intelligent species that was an inevitable outcome on Earth, the effort to colonize Earth had failed. Now they must search elsewhere for another emerging planet that would not violate their ethical directives and would be suitable for them to live. Nevertheless, they lied about their reason for leaving. Their prime directive was to perpetuate their own species without regard to the possible emergence or destruction of any other intelligent species. They disguised the truth by offering the finders of the cube a wonderful 'gift' inside, a gift that would change and advance the discoverer's civilization. The truth was that they designed the cube in such a way that it could only be opened when back on Earth where their seeds could escape. Their so-called gift was a devious means to transport their seeds back to Earth to perpetrate their species."

Jerry paused and took a sip of water as a rumble spread throughout the audience.

"I was at the Yucca Mountain Research Labs when the Dorian cube disintegrated and exposed the sphere within. The sphere contained a gelatinous substance consisting of thousands of nucleated alien cells, each containing viable Dorian DNA. This was the first sign of living alien life ever discovered by humans, and the UWSF scientists decided to nurture and study those cells in an ill-advised and dangerous experiment. They claimed the Yucca Mountain facility is safe to conduct such an experiment, and in no way would those alien cells ever escape their labs. Dr. Vincent and I were not convinced and argued they must destroy those seeds. Because of my insistence, the director ordered me to keep silent about the alien cells. Until this lecture, I have done so. Even as I speak, those alien cells are being nurtured and grown inside their lab at Yucca Mountain and the danger of their escape remains real. Our team leader, Dr. Josh Vincent, couldn't be here today but he recently viewed this experiment and his concern grows even stronger every day."

The audience erupted, not with applause but with a clamor for Jerry to answer questions.

The first question was why they did not have recorded evidence of the Dorian holographic projection. Jerry explained that none of their instruments was able to record this event.

"Very convenient," someone in the audience said.

They asked why the cube had disintegrated in the Yucca Mountain lab. Jerry explained that as designed, the cube would only open in the presence of Earth's gravity. After several other questions, most of which questioned Jerry's veracity, he had said enough and left the podium. Wendy pushed through the crowd and gave Jerry a big hug as he exited the auditorium. "Hang in there," she whispered in his ear.

The next morning Jerry tried to contact Josh, but his wife said he had been detained.

"Detained … by whom?" Jerry asked.

She didn't know. "Some government agency at Yucca Mountain," was all that she could say.

The next day the media blazed with various accounts of Jerry's lecture. The UWSF wasted no time in discounting Jerry and his claims naming him a liar and attention-seeker. They even claimed that he had not even been in the lab when they opened the cube. Everyone was trying to contact Josh but he didn't return calls and no one knew where he was. The media contacted Wendy and Dr. Mitera who backed up everything Jerry had said about Sedna, the Dorian archives, the holographic message, and the cube, but only Josh could back up Jerry's claims about the alien cells.

Jerry harbored no illusions about what had happened to Josh. He was certain the USWF was holding him at Yucca Mountain. He tried to contact him but Josh's satellite phone had been turned off.

True to Dr. Ingram's threat, the following day the UC Berkeley chancellor called and fired Jerry with no specific reason given. He allowed that Jerry could remove personal items from his office but only under armed escort.

"So, what do we do now?" Carol asked. "How will we live and how can we afford Aden's tuition at Stanford?"

"Not to worry," Jerry answered. "I intend to publish a book, and there is always the lecture tour. In fact, Bill Summerset called and offered me a job in his meteorite lab. How would you feel about moving to Arizona?"

"Now that you mentioned Bill's name, several years ago a package arrived for you from the University of Arizona. I had totally forgotten about it." Carol dug around in Jerry's office and recovered the package still wrapped in brown paper and tape. Jerry tore off the paper and opened the container. Inside was the meteorite he lent to Bill eight years ago.

He handed the potato-size pit scarred meteorite to Carol who repeatedly turned the rock over in her hands. She wasn't impressed.

"It's just like the other rocks you have stacked on that shelf and not as beautiful or interesting as most," she said as she pointed to the wall shelf loaded with various rocks, geodes, and minerals.

Jerry took the meteorite from her hands and cleared a prominent place for it on the shelf.

"Wrong.... This little rock is unique," Jerry said as he adjusted its position to catch the maximum amount of light. "This meteorite may not be pretty, and in fact could even be considered ugly, but it is very a special rock. It is over seven billion years old and came from another far-flung star system. It took eons to arrive here and is a rare alien visitor to our solar system."

Jerry sat down, smiled, and said, "And like the Dorians, it never belonged in our solar system or on our planet."

The End

www.ingramcontent.com/pod-product-compliance
Lightning Source LLC
Chambersburg PA
CBHW050539190726
48284CB00003B/1142